UPON A MIDNIGHT CLEAR

M.J. Schiller

Published by Kissmet Publishing

PROLOGUE

Max didn't expect the explosion. He heard the tremendous, almost rhythmic sound of metal crunching as the car cartwheeled down the side of the cliff like a preschooler at recess. The thunderous *BOOM* of the sedan going up in flames caught him by surprise. He rushed to peer over the edge, but the blast shook the ground and he froze for a second. By the time he got to the side of the ridge, the fire had already engulfed the vehicle. The flames licked hungrily at the night sky like so many devils' tongues and consumed the car with such vehemence that, within seconds, only a black outline of the frame remained.

Looking back on it, standing on the side of the road was an incredibly stupid thing to do. Anyone could have seen him as they whizzed up the side of the mountain, perhaps even noting the dents in his car and copying down the license plate number. But he wanted to see the results of his handiwork. Besides, he wasn't thinking at all clearly that night.

It had given him a raw thrill to chase the sedan over the edge of the cliff. He'd followed Kevin home from work, desperate, not knowing what he would do to solve his problem. At first he had only picked up speed to keep pace with Kevin, but then recklessness had pumped in his veins. He'd pulled out into the lane meant for oncoming traffic, not even realizing what he was doing. His eyes had darted everywhere, and his pulse had raced; he was frightened witless as the scenery flew by. Luckily, for some reason, the usually well-travelled road lay deserted. Perhaps thinking he wanted to pass him, Kevin had slowed down, no doubt cursing the crazy driver beside him. But Max only matched the sedan's speed. Kevin glanced over, and in the flash of a streetlight, seemed to recognize him.

He must have thought ol' Max didn't have it in him. But I did.

He remembered the changing expressions on Kevin's face as he began to understand his adversary's intentions. At first his brow had been furrowed in confusion. Then his jaw went rigid and he tightened his grip on the wheel, glaring at Max, who feinted with his car. Kevin had to swerve onto the shoulder before correcting the path of the sedan. That was when Max's prey stared back, his eyes hollowed by fear. A wild laugh burst through the air and Max wondered at first where it came from, before realizing it belonged to him.

The vehicles jostled, and tires screeched. When Kevin's car finally did careen over the edge of the cliff, Max could have sworn he felt the heat of the gigantic explosion, although he knew that was impossible. For him it was like an orgasm, a wave of pleasure and relief. Kevin Kelly was no more.

If only that had been the end of it.

CHAPTER ONE

Dylan Fischer wiped the sweat from underneath his fake eyebrows. As if it weren't hot enough in his jolly, red suit, today it seemed like the mall's heating system was cranked up to full blast. He was basting in his own juices, not unlike the Thanksgiving turkey of weeks before.

"Next," an elf called out in a flat tone.

She must be as worn out as I am, Dylan thought sympathetically. *The holidays are getting to us all, I guess.* Dylan stifled a yawn and peered out over the crowd, mentally tallying the length of the line. All the way down to the pretzel place. Not good. Bringing his eyes back to focus on the little girl approaching him, Dylan heard the elf whispering into his ear the name she received over her walkie-talkie.

You need to wake up, man, Dylan chided himself. This little girl, like all the rest, deserved as special a visit from Santa as he could muster.

She sure was an adorable little thing. The girl brushed her strawberry-blond hair away from her expressive green eyes as she neared. She wore a Christmas-green, velvet dress with a white faux-fur collar and wide, black belt, looking as if she belonged in a magazine ad for a children's boutique. To top it off, under the dress, he now noted, was a pair of candy cane tights. Having reached the bottom of the three steps up to his—you could only call it a throne—the girl turned to glance back over the people gathered outside his little "Winter Wonderland," no doubt trying to find her mom or dad behind the temporary barriers.

Dylan hoped the little girl wasn't the scared-of-Santa type. It made him feel awful when parents forced their kid to sit on his lap and then the child cried the whole time. But when this little girl turned back and their eyes met, the smile she gave Dylan knocked the tired right out of him. He summoned up his best Santa voice.

"Well, well, hello there, little Miss Delaney."

She let out the cutest little gasp at the sound of her name, as if she believed he must be the real deal if he knew that.

"Hello, Santa," she replied, her eyes sparkling.

Dylan judged her to be around six or seven, although she spoke with a certain aged-wisdom which went well beyond her years. He slapped his knee. "Do you want to sit on my lap?"

The girl nodded and he reached to pick her up, ignoring the stab of pain which made his twenty-eight-year-old back feel like the real Kris Kringle's. Between lifting patients on a double shift he'd pulled the night before on his job as a paramedic and reaching for children this afternoon, he was sore. He knew he needed a good, hot shower. Not to mention it would help with the perspiring he was doing under the big lights that had been set up for the camera. *I must smell rank,* he thought with a grin.

"So, Delaney, are you enjoying a little shopping?" The bright-eyed little girl nodded with enthusiasm. "Good. Good. Well, I know you've behaved this year, so, tell me, what is it you want for Christmas, honey?"

Her gaze skimmed over the crowd again and Dylan searched the faces as well, wondering which ones belonged to her parents. Delaney's focus shifted back to him, her face sincere as she crooked a little finger to tell him to come closer, although they were only a breath apart to begin with. He leaned in farther, tickled by her earnestness. He wasn't at all prepared for her whispered request.

"Well, Santa, since my daddy went to heaven, I want a new daddy."

Dylan sat stock still, his heart in his throat. He'd heard kids ask for everything from the newest video games to snow, but this was a new one. He pulled back. "You want...a daddy?" His voice sounded odd in his ears.

The little girl nodded, appearing prayerful as she clasped her hands in front of her, the knuckles turning white. He gazed into her sweet face and began stroking her hair absentmindedly. At a loss, he threw a quick glimpse at his elf assistant. With her head cocked, she listened for the next name in her walkie-talkie, not looking in his direction at all. Scanning the crowd, he hoped to find some inspiration, something he could say to the child on his knee which would somehow be right in this situation.

That's when he saw her face. He knew the woman leaning across the retractable band, waving frantically, must be Delaney's mother. It wasn't so much that she bore a striking resemblance to her daughter, but there was something about her. She possessed the same, round eyes—though the mom's proved a more interesting grey—and warm smile, only with just the thinnest veil of sadness. Or had he perhaps, just imagined it, having seconds before found out she was a widow? He took in her china-pale skin and straight, auburn hair, hanging just to the shoulder. Her bangs made her look a bit like Cleopatra and accented those already fabulous eyes all the more.

He tore his eyes away from the striking face, peering again into the miniaturized version in front of him. "Well, honey, I-I..."

An elf at the bottom of the stairs interrupted him, leaning with one bent leg on an upper step, an elbow on her knee, and fist balled under the chin. "I'm sorry, sweetheart, but Santa needs to visit with some of the other children. Did you get to tell him what you wanted?"

Delaney gazed at Dylan solemnly; the look swore him to secrecy. "Yes. Yes, I did," she replied in that grown-up way of hers, and then she did something unexpected. She kissed him on the cheek and hopped down, slipping her hand into the elf's hand. As they walked away, Delaney glanced back. He sat frozen, his mouth hanging open. An elf leaned in.

"Tommy."

"What?"

She frowned. "Tommy."

Dylan turned to look at her. "Oh, right...Tommy."

KEIRA KELLY'S HEART swelled with warmth for the first time in months. She waved as her daughter, Delaney, whispered something in the mall Santa's ear. It made her want to cry with happiness, and sorrow. Kevin should be here to see this, she couldn't help but think.

Her sister-in-law, Jeanie, reached over to squeeze her hand. "It's hard, isn't it?"

She swallowed and nodded. Hard? Hard didn't even begin to explain it. Right now, Kevin should be the one holding her hand. She could even hear his voice and imagine what he would be saying. She knew the exact proud, satisfied smile he would be wearing. Hell, she almost could smell the familiar scent of his skin wafting through the mall. Her heart felt heavy and tears threatened at the corners of her eyes. She swept the thought from her mind, hiding it away like a Christmas present to be unwrapped later, when she lay awake in her bed.

"I'm sorry, Keira. Maybe this was a bad idea." Jeanie was trying her best to smooth over their first Christmas without Kevin, but nothing was going to help. Eleven months had passed since the car accident took his life, but the ache hadn't seemed to lessen.

At least in returning to her job as a kindergarten teacher Keira had finally begun to be able to put coherent sentences together again. In the beginning, she'd felt like a vital part of her had disappeared that night with Kevin, the part which could think clearly, feel emotion, even sleep and eat. The only thing which got her through that time was knowing Delaney was in the next room. Keenly aware that her little six-year-old heart needed a mother who was present in every way, Keira had pushed on. It scared her sometimes to think about what might have happened if Delaney hadn't been around to pull her out of the darkness of those first several months. Grief threatened to swallow her, but caring for her daughter helped her to rise above it.

"I'm fine," she lied, the words habit now. Maybe if she said them enough, someday they'd be true. She squeezed Jeannie's hand back and turned to smile at her. "Thanks for inviting us out."

"Anytime, Keira. You know that."

She nodded and turned back. Delaney skipped down the ramp toward her holding the elf's hand, face aglow. Keira's nearly six-year-old baby was coming and she needed to get a grip. She blinked back the tears like a pro and took a long, slow breath.

"How'd it go, sweetheart?" Keira crouched down and held her daughter's arms as she talked to her, needing to offer this comforting touch as well as be comforted by it.

"Great!"

"Really? Did you get to tell Santa what you want him to bring?" She glanced up at the elf with a smile.

Delaney nodded.

A glimmer of joy warmed Keira again. She was certain Delaney must have asked for the collectible doll, which she had ordered a month ago and hidden in the basement storage room. It was vital for Delaney to enjoy the best Christmas she could provide. It wasn't fair for them to be spending it without her daddy, so naturally Keira felt responsible for making it up to Delaney somehow. *That's what a mom is supposed to do, right? Kiss away the boo-boos?*

Keira rose. "Thank you," she said with a smile to the elf.

"Our pleasure. Delaney did a great job."

Keira winked at her daughter. "You did?"

Jeannie nudged her. "Here come my two hooligans."

Two towheaded girls were heading toward them with their own elf escorts.

"Well," Keira said, forcing her voice to sound bright, "how would you feel about capping off this outstanding day with a cup of cocoa before we head home?"

Delaney piped up. "Yea!"

"Can you all join us, Jean?"

"For hot chocolate? I don't know. Sugar and Spice here don't care much for hot chocolate, do you?"

"Hot chocolate!" her youngest cried, though her older sister talked over her.

"Mom, come on. You know we like hot chocolate." The twelve-year-old Bella, the Spice of the Sugar and Spice duo, stood with a hand on one hip, head tilted to the side. She looked away from her mom and dropped the frown from her face. "Come on, Laney." She snatched her cousin's hand up and all three kids began skipping down one of the mall's wide aisles. The crowd was thinner away from Santa's throne, giving them room to be rambunctious.

Keira sighed, looking after them. "I don't want this day to end." She smiled at her sister-in-law then watched the girls again. Their laughter floated back to her, but her heart did another little dive. She didn't want this day to end because she didn't want to go home to her empty bed and the house Kevin had never lived in with the two of them.

As an experienced mother she knew, though, she needed to get her daughter home and tucked into bed before too long. So, fifteen minutes later, having said goodbye to their extended family, the pair headed to the mall exit nearest to where they'd parked.

Upon stepping out of the stifling, over-warm mall, the bracing wind was almost a relief. Still, within minutes, Keira was glad she had insisted on zipping up Delaney's coat. She gave her mittened hand a squeeze as they hustled across the parking lot to their SUV. The wind blew Delaney's cotton-white scarf across her face as if trying to protect her from its own blustery nature. Keira glanced down. Delaney must have smiled behind the scarf she wore as the edges lifted with her cheeks, and her eyes crinkled up where they peeked out from under the rim of the hat. It was a good night. Maybe together they would make it through this first Christmas without Kevin...somehow.

Mother and daughter skidded across the parking lot, making tracks in the new kiss of slick snow covering the pavement like a satin sheet. The wind continued to pound into their faces, reddening their cheeks and stealing away the warmth the mall and hot chocolate granted them. When they finally reached their SUV, Delaney scrambled up into a car seat, but then turned to argue with her mother.

"Why can't I sit in the front where Daddy used to?" she asked for the hundredth time.

"Because, Laney," Keira replied with a sigh, acknowledging the stab of pain the comment gave her, and then letting it fade away, "it's the law, remember?" She tweaked the little girl's red nose. "Besides, I like to see you when I look into my rearview mirror." The two of them played this little game together, talking to each other's eyes in the mirror. Delaney smiled at the thought while she snapped the various straps of the car seat over her little one's chest. She paused to lay her wool-encased hand on one sweet, appled cheek. Delaney leaned into her palm for a second or two before Keira slid it down to give her daughter's chin a squeeze. "Let's get outa here." She closed the door to walk around to her side of the SUV.

The crystal-clear Denver sky drew her gaze upward, stars cutting through the inky darkness like sequins on a black party dress. Keira paused. Was Kevin up there, somewhere, looking out for them? She missed Kevin for all of the little things that made him Kevin, but also because she longed to have someone there to share in her love for Laney. Someone to lie awake with at night, discussing the cutest little thing Laney said earlier or the funny thing she did after lunch. Without that adult presence in her life, Keira knew she had become too wrapped up in her daughter. The two of them existed in their own tiny bubble. It wasn't healthy for either of them. She needed to find more balance in her life, but being a single mom and a full-time teacher left little time for self-improvement. She frowned at the stars; they couldn't provide her with the answers she sought.

From the corner of her eye, Keira noticed a car with its headlights on which seemed to be waiting for their spot. She shook herself and quickly got behind the wheel to pull out.

Glancing in the rearview mirror she wondered, idly, why the car didn't take her spot, but rather, continued on behind them.

MAX GERARDI COULDN'T believe his good fortune in finding her. It was like an early Christmas present. She had made it impossible for him by disappearing shortly after the funeral and selling the house. But today Max just happened upon their SUV with the familiar "Stars and Bars Gymnastics Academy" sticker on the back window with "Delaney" under the image of a shooting star. Of all the streets crisscrossing through Denver, he'd turned on theirs to avoid a traffic jam and found them. Truly a Christmas miracle. Not to mention he could have just driven past the SUV without even noticing it, or come two minutes later and missed them. As it was, he had sat outside their little brick home wondering what he should do about his discovery, when he saw her and the little girl leaving the house. On instinct, he followed them to the mall.

Max stewed in his truck for four hours waiting for them to come out, turning the engine on and off to heat up, cursing women for their fickle shopping habits. This time it would pay off for him. The delay gave him enough time to figure out his strategy. Too bad the little girl was with her tonight, he thought, but it couldn't be helped. Max started the engine again, sliding the window open to erase the condensation his breathing created. In his other hand he wadded up a ball of plastic wrap from a sandwich he just finished, left over from lunch. He shoved the trash through the window crack just before it completed its trip back up and eased out of his parking spot.

CHAPTER TWO

Dylan trudged down the lengthy enclosed hallway leading to the employee break room, exhausted beyond measure. His heavy, black boots scraped across the concrete, their thuds creating a dull echo all around him. He reached the door and grabbed the knob, glancing through the half window into the tiny room. Eddy Bender. The portly security guard, was pushed away from the table, his hands folded over his paunch, crumbs from the dinner he had probably just finished still visible on his black tie. The tie was almost comical in the way it didn't come close to his belt buckle, the gap between tie and belt three or four shirt buttons long. The door creaked open.

"Hey, Eddy."

"Hiya, Dylan. How was your night?"

Dylan raised a false eyebrow. "Incredibly busy." He crossed to the lockers to get his gym bag.

Eddy chuckled, his jowls shaking. "Tired, are ya?"

"Beat," he agreed. "I'm beginning to wonder if all this extra work is worth it." He worked on his lock's combination but remained half turned in the older man's direction. "I may get my EMT schooling paid off sooner, but a fat lot of good it'll do me if I end up in the hospital myself, a victim of overwork." When he'd become a paramedic after his father's death it had felt right, like somehow he canceled out the loss of his father by saving others. Lately, though, he was sensing something missing in his life. Helping others at his job was uplifting, but at the end of shift, he returned home, lost to an emptiness that all his lifesaving couldn't fill. It wasn't just the physical exhaustion he felt; he simply needed more in his life.

Eddy sighed. "I hear ya. I hear ya. If the old lady keeps on buying gifts for the grandkids, I may have to put in some extra hours myself." His fingers still locked together, he twiddled his thumbs over his chest, shaking his head a little.

Dylan slung the bag he had retrieved from the locker over his shoulder and closed it, turning to face Eddy. "Come on now. I've seen you with those grandkids of yours. Are you sure it's not *you* buying the presents?" He grinned.

Eddy sat up straight in his chair, the picture of innocence. "Who me? Nah. I ain't getting those brats a damn thing." He busied himself closing up the storage containers on the table that must have contained the meatloaf Dylan was smelling.

"Uh-huh. And that radio-control plane I see in the corner behind you is for you?"

Eddy turned toward the package as if just seeing it for the first time. "What? That? Oh, yeah. Sure. That's for me. Lotta guys my age have 'em." He tried to keep up the charade but his eyes sparkled.

Dylan rested his hands on the back of the chair across from Eddy and leaned forward. "My guess is it's for the oldest one, Richie."

"Nah." He waited a beat and then placed his hands on the table, scooting his chair back a little. "The middle one, Tommy."

"I knew it."

Eddy chuckled, shrugging. He turned to again eye the gift. "It's a beaut. It wouldn't fit in a locker. Do you think it'll be safe here?"

"Of course. We've got an ace security team." Dylan winked.

Eddy rolled his eyes, "Yeah, right." He stood. "Speaking of which, I guess I better go do a swing around the place, seein' as I've been on the clock for about fifteen minutes." He turned with a hand on the doorknob. "What about you? You going home to the little missus?"

"Nah, man. I told you, I'm not married." It wasn't that he didn't want to be. It was just all the girls Dylan dated ended up being either paper mache—pretty, but hollow inside—or they held their own agendas, which generally consisted of his providing for their every whim without giving anything in return. He longed to connect with someone, really *connect*. Build a house. Raise some kids. But Dylan couldn't quite figure out how to make it happen. So he figured he'd just take his time, see how things played out and hope for the best. Lately, that just didn't seem like enough.

Eddy tsked as he opened the door. "Nice kid like you. I don't understand it."

"Yeah. You and my sister-in-law." Dylan followed him out into the hall. "Have a good night."

"You, too, Dylan."

He hadn't even bothered to change in the locker room. He just wanted to hit the sack. He also entertained serious fantasies about a tall, cold Budweiser when he hit the outer door and stepped into the night. Then his fantasy altered slightly and he clinked brown bottles with the redhead he saw in line earlier, the one with the fatherless little girl.

Where did that come from? He chuckled at his fantasy. Another downside to working so much, he admitted, was the lack of female company. He hadn't been with a woman in... longer than he cared to consider, and Dylan blamed that for sending his thoughts soaring back to the pretty face in the crowd like a paper airplane. Who could blame him? She was extremely attractive. Not exactly the model-type, who clearly knows all eyes are on her and relishes the power inherent in it. Instead this woman possessed open, warm, yet still flawless beauty. Of course, this made her even further beyond reach than your average model would be. A model might play games with him, but a woman like that? She would not play any games at all, and would be hard to draw out. He sighed. Why couldn't he meet a girl like her?

A ball of plastic wrap bounced out of a dark pocket in the parking lot and into the spotlight of the overhead lights, looking like a tumble weed as it somersaulted over the ground. It caught on his shoe for a minute before trying to continue on. Aggravated by the unknown litterbug, he bent to snatch it up, his back forcing a groan from his lips. Why were people so lazy they couldn't even make an effort to find one of the many trash cans the mall provided? Snagging it with the tips of his fingers before it rolled off again, he pushed the ball of used wrap through the small opening where his bag hadn't been zipped up all the way, intending to throw it out when he got home.

He arrived at his car, and brushed the snow from the windows with his hands, not worrying about whether or not the white Santa gloves he wore became dirty. Catching a reflection in the glass, Dylan paused mid-swipe, surprised to see his beard still in place, having forgotten he chose not to change. Then Delaney's little voice came whirling through his mind like the snow dervishes by the parking lot's fence, "Well, Santa, since my daddy went to heaven, I want a new daddy." It struck him again, the sweet simplicity of the request, the certainty that somehow he would come through for her.

He held the keys in his hand and shuffled through them by the light from a nearby post, staring at them without really seeing. Where was the little girl right now? Where was Delaney? Had her mom already tucked her in for the night? He could almost see it in his mind. He imagined Delaney underneath some pink, flowery comforter, with a stuffed animal in the crook of each elbow, tucked in with her, their hoofs or paws or whatever, hanging out over the top of the blankets like their owner's little hands. He saw the redhead bending down to give her a soft kiss on the cheek, closing the door with a click, and turning to shuffle down a long hallway to her own bedroom. In his imagination, the woman opened the door at the end of the hall, and the light fanned out on a big, empty bed. She leaned against the door frame, dreading entering the room. Once full of love and laughter, he now imagined it had turned into her private torture chamber.

Dylan shook his head, selecting the right key at last from the jumble in his hand, and sticking it into the door's lock. Throwing his gym bag into the passenger's seat, he slid behind the wheel and started the engine. He blew on his hands, suddenly noticing the cold. He waited for the car to warm up. He couldn't imagine trying to live life with such a hole in it...or could he? At least his hole was nameless, featureless. He put the car into reverse and backed out.

KEIRA GLANCED IN THE rearview mirror and noted her daughter's heavy eyelids. From experience she knew if Delaney fell asleep now, when they were only ten minutes from home, her little sweetheart would be a bear to deal with when she got her out of her car seat. Delaney as deadweight was almost too much for her to handle now; not to mention juggling keys and manipulating doorknobs. And if she woke her up to get her to walk, she would be a huge crab. She needed to keep her awake for the duration of the ride.

Snapping off the radio, which warbled a Christmas carol at low volume, she used Laney's nickname, "How about we sing our own Christmas song, Bear?"

"Okay," Delaney responded listlessly, her head still turned toward the window, which was too fogged up to see out of.

"What do you want to sing?" When she got no response, Keira launched into "Jingle Bells," desperate to keep her daughter awake. To her relief, after a few measures, Delaney's sweet little voice chimed in, weakly at first, but growing more alert. She smiled into the rearview mirror as Laney's eyes met hers. *That a girl.* She pulled the SUV onto First Avenue and picked up speed to match the busy thoroughfare while "laughing all the way" with Delaney.

Keira glanced over to the left as an uneasy feeling crept over her. The car in the next lane had matched her pace for too long a distance and it was creeping her out. The driver of a black sedan, a nondescript, middle-aged man dressed in business attire, faced her. Keira couldn't be sure if he intended to look at her in the dark, but, in any case, the man turned his head away almost immediately and stared at the road.

She checked her rearview mirror again and launched into "Frosty the Snowman." Delaney seemed to like this song even better and belted out the lyrics, or a close proximity to the lyrics, in a cute, off-key kind of way.

Out of the corner of her eye, Keira noticed the black car impinging on her lane. Directing her attention again to the other driver, she wondered if he was drunk. She decided to speed up and get the car safely behind her where she could keep tabs on him in the mirrors. But, to her annoyance, the driver revved his engine along with hers, remaining beside the SUV as she increased speed. Glancing over a second time, she could see the driver leaning forward now, sort of hunched over the wheel, gripping it with two hands, his head turned in her direction. She scowled, wondering why he seemed to want to play games with her. She slowed, while at the same time searching for an opportunity to switch lanes.

Within seconds, she saw the chance, and moved over to the far right lane, only to have her antagonist move over, too. *What the hell*? Her heart began to beat faster. She was no longer singing, but Delaney didn't seem to even notice, carrying on without her. She heard her singing about Frosty "hippity-hop-hopping through the snow."

Keira was pretty sure that was wrong, (didn't Peter Rabbit "hippity-hop?"), but didn't bother to correct Delaney. Her hands clutched the steering wheel as she hunted for a street ahead they could turn down. Spotting one, she waited until the last minute to signal and then made a right-hand turn. To her horror, tires screeched and beams from the black sedan's headlights swung crazily as the car swerved around the corner, too, fish-tailing in the snow, but following all the same. A motor raced as it zoomed up on them, getting so close she lost sight of its headlights as they dipped below the SUV's back bumper.

Her heart thudded in her chest. *I can't panic. Kevin told me if someone ever followed me I should head straight to a police station. But where's a police station*? She searched her mind, street names and places flashing before her eyes and then the impact of the sedan's bumper jolted the SUV.

"Mommy!" Delaney screamed.

"It's okay, sugar." Even though she wanted to sound reassuring, her voice was tight. The car rammed them again.

"Mommy!"

Keira's eyes flew back and forth from the rearview mirror to the road, trying to remain in control of the vehicle and anticipate her attacker's next move at the same time. The street she'd chosen was dark. A park hemmed either side of the two-lane road and a long row of drivers in the opposite lane waited their opportunity to turn onto First Avenue.

"Aah!" She involuntarily yelped as the sedan hit them with greater impact, making her SUV skid across the pavement. She quickly corrected and then tried to speed up to avoid another collision. She checked the side view mirror. Headlights zoomed up again and she braced herself.

Too late, Keira saw the car in front of her making a leisurely left-hand turn onto the thoroughfare from a side street. She screamed and slammed on the brakes. The SUV began to skid sideways, her rear bumper making contact with one of the cars waiting in line next to them, sending her vehicle spinning in the opposite direction. Delaney's cries rang in her ears. Images blurred through the windshield, a tree, a lamp post, and then, the car gunning for them. With a tremendous crash of metal, it drove the SUV into a park bench and a concrete, cylinder-shaped garbage receptacle decorated with neutral-colored pebbles. The airbags failed to deploy. Her head hit the steering wheel with the initial impact, and then the side window when the SUV crumpled against the pebbled trash can.

A car horn blared, her car horn. She struggled to lift her head. About ten feet in front of them, the black sedan swam in and out of her vision. Its front bumper trailed on the ground on one side, half of the hood accordioned upward, steam rolling out of it menacingly in the cold night air. She imagined the black vehicle to be some sort of fire-breathing dragon. *Why does it want me dead?*

It came to life in front of her eyes, backing up over the curb a few feet, pieces clunking and scraping against the concrete. The wheels turned and with a screech of spinning tires it scrambled toward her. For a minute, she thought it sought to finish them off. Instead, the sedan roared off into the night with sparks flying from its underbelly.

Pardoned for the moment, she became aware of the pain driving through her brain. The metallic taste of blood invaded her mouth and she clutched her stomach against a sickening pain. Head heavy, she laid it down on the steering wheel, closing her eyes. She heard the horn again...shouting... somewhere, Christmas music.

Delaney! Keira wanted to turn to search the back seat, but it felt like her head was no longer connected to the rest of her body. She heard a strange noise, a loud, screeching, whirring noise...the dragon returning. She whimpered and gave into the blackness.

CHAPTER THREE

Traffic along First Avenue seemed to be at a crawl. Dylan wondered what the holdup could be at this time of night, and decided to cut through the park. A siren headed in his direction. That explained it.

The ambulance struggled getting through traffic and from his angle he saw a pretty clear shot to the accident scene, with a little creative driving. One good thing about having a piece of crap for a car, you never worried about damaging it. Dylan steered onto the curb, riding the fifteen feet to the intersection while tilted at an angle, ignoring all the looks and curse words thrown at him as he avoided hazards such as trees and fire hydrants.

"What the hell, Santa?" some guy yelled out his window.

He had a strong urge to flip the guy off, but felt obliged to uphold the image of the red suit in case any kids spotted him. After several minutes, he arrived at the crumpled up SUV. The brunt of the damage to the SUV seemed to be to the middle of the vehicle, where it met up with one very immovable trash can. No one was near the vehicle and there were no footprints in the snow. He hopped out, leaving his engine running and lights on.

He reached the door of the vehicle, noting a woman slumped over the steering wheel. The shoulder-length, red hair looked familiar. He stepped up on the remains of the park bench and put a hand to the glass of the rear window to cut the glare, leaning in to search the back seat. He spotted the empty car seat and light streaming in from the open door on the other side.

Lifting his eyes, he located the little girl, Delaney, in the arms of an elderly man parked across the street. The man—tall and thin, with curly, grey hair and a thick mustache, darker than the hair on his head—made him think of Samuel Clemens. He wore a long, black dress coat and leather gloves and drove a dark-colored luxury sedan. A woman, most likely his wife, joined the Sam Clemens lookalike, her purple coat standing out like a beacon against the white snow. The woman leaned in to talk to Delaney, patting her arm, but she was hysterical, shaking and crying. The little girl turned her head, catching his eyes. She froze in disbelief, her mouth hanging open. Dylan swallowed. The poor thing lost her father, and now, her mother might be badly hurt.

Please let her be hurt and not—

Tearing his eyes away from Delaney, he yanked on the front door handle of the SUV. The lock was engaged, but he doubted the beaten up door would hold for long. He struggled to make enough clearance for the door to open, pushing back against the twisted metal of the bench, and letting the snow work in his favor to slide the vehicle away some. The ambulance made its way to the scene, driving as he had, along the curb. The EMTs rolled a stretcher and equipment his way, but stopped when they saw Kris Kringle beside the damaged SUV.

"I'm an EMT!" Dylan shouted, and the pair nodded, again rushing toward him. He gave the door one last jerk and was rewarded when something snapped, and the metal gave way with a loud creak and groan. *Please let her be breathing...just let her be breathing.* Taking great care, he pulled the woman back toward the seat, her head lolling to one side. Her chest rose and fell with quick shallow breaths. She bore a nasty gash above one eye, which bled profusely, and another on her chin. Her mouth was swollen as well, but he still felt a tug in his groin as he stared into the captivating face, now so deathly pale. Ignoring his hormonal reaction, he called to the EMT's who had just reached them. "Gauze." Reaching into his kit, the taller of the two, an African American male who looked all of twenty-one, tossed him a roll. Dylan ripped it open with his teeth, discarding the packaging in the interior of the vehicle and checking for any broken glass before pressing it to the girl's head. The windshield remained intact, and so had the side window—a miracle, considering it was laced with spider-webbed cracks from where the woman's head had hit. A second EMT, who appeared to be older, maybe in his early thirties, stocky with short brown hair, ducked under Dylan's arm and squatted, pulling out his own pad of gauze and pressing it to the victim's lip. Recognizing the territorial look in the man's eyes, Dylan backed off slightly, but continued to apply pressure to the cut above his patient's eye. The woman began to come around, moaning and moving her head a little from side to side.

"Ma'am? Ma'am?" The EMT shifted as he spoke, revealing a name tag above his badge that read Bob Westfelder. "You need to stay still."

The woman's eyes fluttered open and she seemed disoriented for a second before becoming agitated. "Delaney? Delaney!" Her gaze flew to the rearview mirror that dangled overhead at an odd angle. Not that it mattered, since the child she was looking for wasn't there.

The EMT tried to gently restrain the distraught mother. "What? What's that?" He tried to look past her shoulder to the back of the vehicle.

Dylan ignored him. "She's okay." He gestured with his head to the other side of the street. Delaney still struggled in the arms of the older man, who seemed bent on keeping her away from the scene.

The injured woman's head swiveled, with effort, in that direction. "Oh," she sighed, the lines relaxing on her forehead as she sank back into her seat. Her eyes closed and he could see the tension in her jaw from pain and wished he was performing the assessment her condition. He managed to keep his yap shut while the EMT, who seemed quite good really, examined the woman and asked her questions. She answered, fairly coherently, but her responses kept getting weaker. After a few minutes, her eyes popped open as if remembering something, and they focused on Dylan.

His chest clutched as those troubled grey eyes leveled on him. Her lips curled up at the edges, but her eyes closed again, tired from the exertion of doing even that. "Santa rescued me?"

He smiled, a surge of relief warmed him even in the bitter cold and the EMTs also chuckled at her off-beat response. They braced her neck with a C-collar as a precautionary measure. Dylan stayed with her until they removed her from the vehicle and secured her on a long board and then a stretcher, lending a hand when he could. He glanced across the street and saw the older man hand Delaney to his wife. The man crossed the street as they wheeled the stretcher toward the waiting back of the ambulance. He looked to Dylan for some reason, not seeming to question why the man in the Santa suit had assisted the EMTs.

"How is she?"

"Good, considering," Dylan responded, gesturing to the SUV over his shoulder.

The older man took a peek and visibly shuddered at the sight of the wreckage from the front. He turned back, his eyes wide, jaw tense. Assessing the young woman on the stretcher's face in the light of the open ambulance doors, he hesitated. "Can her little girl come over? She's been asking for her." Dylan raised his eyes to the other EMT's, not wanting to overstep his bounds.

"Sure, for a minute," Bob Westfelder responded. He turned to his patient, touching her on the shoulder so she would know he addressed her. "What's your name, hon?"

She moaned and Bob looked at his partner, who adjusted the IV a little. "Keira. Keira Kelly."

"I'm Samuel Wexford," said the older man. He turned and nodded to his wife, who set Delaney down. As soon as the patent-leather shoes hit the ground, the little girl raced over.

The younger medic, Tony Davis, held out a hand to stop Delaney before she launched herself on the stretcher. "You need to be careful, honey. Your mommy is going to be a little sore," he explained, softening his tone. Delaney's eyes went wide. "But she'll be just fine after we take her to see the doctors," Tony reassured her.

More cautious now, Delaney approached the stretcher. Seeming to sense her daughter near, Keira opened her eyes. "Lane. Laney-girl, come here," she called out with more energy than she had shown before.

"Mommy!" Delaney buried her head in her mother's chest and Keira's arms came up reflexively to hold her daughter, dragging the tubing attached to the IV.

"Are you okay, Lane?"

Delaney lifted her head and nodded vigorously, but as her eyes roamed over her mommy's beaten up face, the little girl began to cry. She reached out a tiny hand and floated it above the corner of Keira's mouth where there was still some bleeding as though afraid to touch her. "Oh, Mommy."

"No, don't cry, Laney-bear. Mommy's just fine. These nice men here are going to help me..." Keira swept her eyes over the faces circled around them and all of the men nodded their agreement.

From out of nowhere, a police officer appeared around one of the open doors of the ambulance, holding a pad of paper in one hand, and writing on it with the other, as if just finishing up some notes. "Ma'am, I'm going to need to ask you some questions." His voice sounded tired and somewhat disgruntled, as if ready to launch into a lecture with her over disrupting his night. All of the other men bristled, several laying a hand on the stretcher in a defensive manner.

Dylan had seen it before. When a woman or child lay injured, an instinct awoke within men to shield them from anything that might be considered harmful. His own surge of protectiveness for Keira and Delaney pitched as the callous cop stood over them. "Can't this wait? They've just been through a huge trauma. Mrs. Kelly needs medical attention and would be hard-pressed to answer any questions with the ringing in her head I'm sure she's experiencing right now."

Keira smiled up at him, her storm-grey eyes warmed. The cop eyed Dylan as if seeing him for the first time, and not liking what he saw. A corner of his lips curled up and his nose wrinkled as if catching a repugnant odor. He thumped Dylan on the chest with the butt of his pen. "Listen, *St. Nick*—"

"I agree." Bob Westfelder cut in. His abrupt statement effectively ended all debate on the matter. Dylan wasn't sure, but he got the strong feeling Westfelder and the cop were acquainted and had perhaps even gotten into it before. Bob glared at him before bending down to Delaney. "How would you like to ride in an ambulance? Not many girls your age get to do that?"

She nodded, giving him a shy smile.

Bob's eyes shifted to Keira to explain. "I'd like to have her checked out. She looks fine. Her side of the vehicle wasn't damaged at all, but just to play it safe."

"That's a good idea," she agreed, and with that they lifted the stretcher and then Delaney into the back of the ambulance.

When the doors closed, the officer started in on Bob, again waving his pen around aggressively. "You know, you're not making my job any easier. I could have you arrested for interfering with an investigation," he added as if just thinking of it.

Bob finished stowing his equipment in a side bin, all but ignoring the policeman's tirade. "You do that."

"Hey," the man called after Bob, who was marching up to the front of the vehicle now to get behind the wheel. "These witnesses," he gestured vaguely, "say someone did this to her on purpose. Do you want to be responsible if he comes after her again? I'm just trying to catch the bastard. Or maybe you don't give a damn what happens to her and the kid—"

Dylan, heading to his car alongside the EMT, saw a spark light in Bob's eyes as he raised his head, reminding the younger man of a lit match falling in midair toward a puddle of gasoline. Bob spun on his heel and charged hotly back toward the police officer. Recognizing the foolhardiness of taking on a cop, no matter how ignorant the guy was, Dylan hurried to step between them.

"Listen, that little girl and her mom are *my* patients and I decide what's best for them."

Dylan, surprised by Bob's strength as he braced his hands against the shorter man's shoulders, had to really dig into the ground and throw his weight forward to keep the pair separated. The policeman, a good head taller than his adversary, seemed hell-bent on starting a fight with him.

"Is that so? Well maybe you should—"

"This isn't helping anybody!" Dylan found himself shouting. He turned his head while still holding Bob back by the shoulders. "You'll get your answers at the hospital. We don't know what kind of internal injuries this woman could have." It was true. Sure the exam gave no hint of any problems, but grave injuries weren't always obvious.

The police officer hesitated, not seeming to have a comeback at first. "Well, you can bet if some guy smashed up her car with all these witnesses around, well, if he got hold of her, *he'd* make damn sure she had some internal injuries, *girls*," he taunted.

Dylan gritted his teeth. He hated this kind of attitude. When things worked right, policemen and paramedics were tight. Paramedics needed policemen to protect them while they worked in volatile situations, or even just to keep the crowd back so they could assess patients without interruption. And God help the policeman who didn't have a paramedic around when he ended up with a bullet in his chest. Most of the time they looked out for one another, but every once in a while, he'd run into a jerk like this who believed anyone who wasn't a cop was less than a man, especially guys working on a rig "nursing" victims.

The cop stomped off and Dylan dropped his hands. Bob Westfelder hissed out a breath and rubbed his eyes with one hand stretched over the bridge of his nose. "Thanks. Battling that tank wouldn't have done my patients any good. I shouldn't be such a hot-head."

"No problem." He and Bob lifted their heads at the same time to peer around the back of the ambulance. Their antagonist returned to his partner, who was still talking to bystanders and taking notes. "Who is he?"

"Officer Gary Leake," the paramedic responded, his jaw tight. "As in, 'I wish you'd go take a leak.'" Bob sighed, and they turned to again head toward the front of the vehicle.

Dylan turned with him, rubbing his fake beard. "Since you've got to get on your way, maybe I could give him a poke or two for you..."

Bob laughed, giving him a fake jab to the shoulder. "Not while you're wearing the suit, Big Man. There could be kids around."

He glanced down, frowning. "Oh, yeah." He jerked his head to the rear of the ambulance. "So where are you taking her?"

Bob opened the driver's side door and climbed up into the rig as he talked to him. "Rocky Mountain Hospital. What was your name again?" He offered his hand before he closed the door.

"Dylan Fischer."

"Right. Nice work, Dylan. And thanks for your help."

He nodded. "Anytime."

Dylan sauntered back to his car, thinking about all that happened. Someone tried to run Delaney and her mom off the road on purpose? Road rage? Whoever he was, surely the cops would get him with this many witnesses. He glanced their way once more. Even cops with pea-sized brains like his.

As he clunked his ramshackle car down off the curb, the policeman and his partner both glanced up. Officer Leake scowled at him and appeared to be mentally writing him a ticket for reckless driving. Dylan rolled down the window, waving as he shouted out through the night,

"HO, HO, HO." He chuckled, checking the rearview mirror and catching sight of Officer Leake's face. It was as red as his Santa suit.

CHAPTER FOUR

Dylan hadn't even questioned himself over staying at the hospital overnight. He'd just wanted to keep tabs on the girl, Keira. That's all. He'd done it on occasion, helped out at an accident scene and come in the next day to monitor the progress of a victim. Of course, in those cases the patient had usually sustained serious injury and he wanted to verify their status. More often than not, he just called in. No, if he wanted an honest answer he'd have to say he stayed around to check on Keira Kelly for another reason.

He'd followed the ambulance to the hospital. Knowing it would take a while to check her in, he headed for the staff showers, which the paramedics were allowed to use on occasion. Dylan finally got out of the Santa suit, showered, and changed into jeans and a t-shirt from his gym bag. After that, he found a room to take a nap in.

When he woke, he asked for Keira's room number and found her. The door was open, but she was asleep. He stared at her, taking in a big breath. *What am I doing?* He glanced up and down the hall for some reason. No one was around.

He entered the room slowly, standing several feet away from her bed with his hands jammed in his pockets. The room was still. Outside in the hallway the usual noises of the hospital carried on—hushed conversations, soft, rhythmic beeping of heart monitors, and overhead pages. He shifted his weight and looked around the room. Nothing special. Sterile, without an ounce of personality. His eyes landed on the chart at the end of the bed and he threw a look over his shoulder. The hallway remained empty so he stepped forward and picked up the chart, but before flipping it open, he again eyed the doorway. *I don't know why I keep feeling like I'm prying into something personal here. I'm a professional. This is what I do.*

Maybe it's because you are taking more than a professional interest here, another voice said, but he silenced it. His focus was drawn to the patient's name at the top of the page. Keira Kelly. It suited her. Like a woodland sprite. He chuckled and glanced up. She hadn't moved. Returning his attention to the chart, he scanned the first page and lifted it to view the next, forgetting to look around as he became absorbed in the information.

A movement drew his attention away. Keira's foot wiggled under the blankets. His gaze traveled over the bed from her toes to her face. "Laney," she said clearly. Her brow was pinched. She turned her head toward the doorway and called out in a more agitated way, "Laney!"

Dylan fumbled as he tried to stash the chart but managed to get it hung on its hook before he rushed to her bedside. Her eyes were closed. He saw her chest rise under the covers, her hand resting lifeless on the sheets. He checked the monitors. Everything normal. He stood watching her, again stabbing his hands into his jeans pockets and resisting the urge to brush the hair out of her face.

After a bit, he grabbed a chair from near the doorway and carried it to within a few feet of the bed, setting it down quietly, watching her face for any reaction, but seeing none. He sat down, elbows on the armrests, hands folded together.

"Kevin!"

At her sharp cry, Dylan inhaled sharply and forced his eyes open. He must have dozed off. How long had he been out? His stomach dropped as he sat forward. She was quiet again. Instinct had him checking the monitors. She was fine. She moaned and moved her head from side to side. He stood and grasped the top of the bed rail, looking down on her. Another moan. He felt his palms begin to sweat. This part of the job he'd never gotten used to, seeing people in agony.

It was what caused him to get into the field in the first place. A year after he finished up college, his dad received a diagnosis that would change everything forever. Bone cancer. Watching him suffer, and being helpless to alleviate it, had almost driven Dylan crazy. He wanted to know more so he could do more. In the end, despite all of his training, it turned out nothing could be done anyway, except to make his father more comfortable. He died a year later.

Dylan slowly lowered himself back into his seat and inhaled. He folded his hands again and waited.

KEIRA PEELED HER EYES open through the horrendous pain, even though the blaring light would be agonizing again. She saw him, swimming in and out of focus. She concentrated on the face, but then it changed to a man with a snowy-white beard. "Santa?"

The man chuckled. "Yeah, I guess so."

"Mmm..."

"You still seem to be in a lot of pain. Let me call a nurse and get you some meds." He reached for the buzzer on her tray but her hand came down on his more quickly than she would have imagined possible, given her condition.

"Please," she begged, her voice coming out scratchy at first. "If you do that, they'll make me stay longer. I have to get back to my daughter. Her father...my husband, died several months ago and... she's all I have...I'm all she has." She blinked back tears, angry she might cry in front of this stranger. But she couldn't help it. All she could think about was getting home with Delaney. Jeanie had taken her home to rest, promising to return once Delaney was settled with the sitter. "Do you understand?" She prayed he would.

His face contorted, lips twitching as if he were struggling with some sort of internal debate. "I shouldn't...if you're not truthful with your doctors you could end up having some condition which will put you back in the hospital eventually, and for a longer time." He paused, but then sighed. "But, I'll admit, it's unlikely. You probably have a concussion. Is that what the doctor said?"

She nodded, seeing some hope. "A mild one."

"Hmm," he commented as if not quite believing her. He pushed the hair away from the bandage on her head to try to get a glimpse at it. His gesture seemed oddly intimate and she drew back a little. Why did this Santa Claus come to see her? The stranger, who she couldn't help but notice was very good-looking, must have seen her reaction because he added, "I'm a paramedic." She relaxed a fraction. "Did they stitch you up?"

She nodded again, though trying not to move because he still attempted to examine her. With a hint of sexy stubble, he was so close she could smell his cologne, something clean and light. Did he stay here all night? "Twenty-six up there and ten on my chin," she answered, nerves making her voice pitch. "Do you think they'll scar?" She didn't like to think herself vain, but she worried about that a little.

He rested his hand on her pillow, apparently considering the question, still leaning in. Now she caught a new smell, mint. He must have been chewing gum earlier. "Who did it?"

"Huh?" She was a little undone by his proximity. He wore a grey t-shirt which stretched across his muscular chest and did something magical to his hazel eyes, setting them dancing in the fluorescent lights.

"The sutures. Who sewed you up?"

"Oh. A Dr. Shapiro, I think he said."

His thoughtful frown disappeared, replaced by an easy grin. "Oh, you should be good then. He's one of the best."

Keira studied him, wondering again why he had come. "I saw you at the accident last night, right?" He nodded. "Thank you for stopping to help. You were...wearing a Santa costume, weren't you?"

"Yes. I'm one of the mall Santas at Cherry Creek."

"Ahh. When you're not working as a paramedic."

"Exactly."

She thought about this. "Delaney must have sat on your lap, then."

"She did." He broke eye contact, shifting his weight as if uneasy, but before she could explore why, a nurse strode in.

"Hey, Brenda."

"Hey, Dylan. What are you doing down in this neck of the woods? I thought you worked in Englewood?"

"I do. I do. But I happened upon an accident scene on my way home from the mall last night and wanted to check on Mrs. Kelly."

"Keira," she suggested. Surely they should be on a first name basis. They had been through so much together, she justified.

"I see," the matronly nurse replied. Her curly, blond hair had been pulled up into a loose bun. She looked between them with confusion at first, and then gave a knowing smile as she took Keira's pulse.

"What?" he asked, also seeming to have noticed the smile.

"Oh. Nothing," the nurse replied, but a slight smile played on her lips. "Well, you're looking good, young lady. You should be out of here in no time." She patted Keira's arm. "I brought your pain meds." Setting a small paper cup on her tray, she reached to fill up a glass with water from a nearby pitcher.

"I don't need any," Keira blurted out.

"What?" The nurse raised her eyebrows in surprise. "You've got a pretty good lump there. Are you telling me you have no headache?"

She squirmed under the nurse's stare. "A little one," she admitted, feeling that was the safest route. "But I'm feeling much better. I think I could go home now."

"Hmmm," the nurse commented, still eyeing her. She leaned in, her face tightening, her voice almost a growl. "Take your pills."

Desperate, Keira's gaze flew to Dylan's.

"Say, Brenda..." He looped a hand over the nurse's shoulder and walked toward the door with her. "Who's on Mrs. Kelly's case?" He winked at Keira over his shoulder.

She lost the conversation as the two left the room but held on to the hope the wink offered. Feeling incredibly tired and having no one to pretend for, she laid her head down again and closed her eyes, just for a second. She wondered if this is how Kevin suffered when his car crashed into the rocky side of the cliff. It still bothered her, the thought Kevin may have been awake and felt the fire. She didn't want to imagine him in pain.

"Ms. Kelly."

She raised her eyelids a fraction to find the police officer from the night before standing at the foot of her bed, gleaming at her like the feline who lunched on the little, yellow bird, obviously happy to have found her alone.

DYLAN KNEW KEIRA STILL suffered from agonizing pain, though she refused to take medication. Well, he'd see about that after he got her discharged.

Little Nurse Brenda told him Dr. Carrie Umbridge was on duty. He and Carrie had dated months ago, and while normally he would consider using a woman's feelings lower than low, in this case the ends justified the means. And Carrie, well, Carrie just had issues.

"Carrie."

"Well, hello there, Handsome." The tall, leggy blonde pulled him into an intimate embrace and, just like that, he felt cheap. "What are you doing here?"

"He came to see the pretty redhead in 401."

Dylan glared at his betrayer and she mouthed, "What?" behind Carrie's back, seeming genuinely confused.

"Did you now?" the good doctor questioned, drawing out her words. She turned her back to the nurses' station, elbows resting on top of the counter behind her, eyeing him with such intensity he could see the vein pulsing at her temple. He'd witnessed that same look on a number of occasions in the days right before their break up. It usually preceded a monumental tizzy fit which usually preceded broken glass, or the necessity of having part of his body stitched up by the person who created the injury. He studied her, his palms sweating now, as she tapped a metal chart up and down in her palm.

"Yeah. You see she has a little girl and her husband—"

"She's *married*?" she practically screeched, standing straighter and gripping the chart until her knuckles blanched.

Dylan turned the doctor down the last time she came on to him for that very reason. "Call me crazy," he'd told her, "but I don't date married women." She hadn't taken it well. He kept his eye on the chart.

"No. No. She's a widow. Her little girl sat on my lap when I was doing my Santa thing at the mall."

"Oh, you played Santa?" a new intern cooed.

"Uh...yeah," he responded, caught off guard by the way the intern was ogling him. As he turned toward her, he caught sight of Officer Leake over the intern's shoulder. The policeman slid into Keira's room. "Anyway, Carrie," he sped up, turning back to her, "she's a widow and wants to get back home to her kid so I'm begging you to try to do the best you can to get her out of here as soon as possible. For her kid, you know?" He hoped she bought it. While she sat deliberating, he couldn't help but fume, "And now that prick Leake is in there questioning her."

"Leake? You mean Gary Leake?" She said the name with venom in her voice, and Dylan remembered he heard she'd been seeing an older cop, and the break up hadn't gone well.

"Yeah."

Carrie stormed past him without another word and he turned to follow in her wake.

As they entered the room, Leake was saying, "You mean to tell me you don't know anyone who might want to see you dead? You're not sneaking around with a married man or anything?"

"No," Keira grimaced, closing her eyes and raising a hand to massage a temple.

"Officer Leake." Carrie pounced, her voice as sharp as the needles in the red hazardous materials disposal box behind her. "This woman is too sick to be questioned."

The big man took a step backward, raising his hands in a defensive gesture, notebook and pen in the air, "Now, Carrie..." He kept the chart under close surveillance, just as Dylan had.

"You heard me. Now get your sorry ass out of here." She picked up the chart at the end of the bed and studied it as if her dismissal was all that was needed.

Keira stared at them both, her eyes wide as if in shock. She looked at Dylan, who shrugged, unable to hide his amusement.

"All right," the policeman huffed. "I'll leave." He hit Keira's toes with his notebook. "But one of these days, when you don't have anyone around running interference for you, you're going to have to answer my questions."

"Are you kidding?" Carrie spat. "Are you *threatening* my patient right in front of me?"

"No. No," Leake responded, skirting her and hurrying out of the room.

"Humpf." Carrie smirked, obviously pleased with herself. She hung the chart on a hook at the end of the bed, sending it swinging. Glancing over her shoulder, presumably to make sure the police officer was out of hearing, she added, "Mrs. Kelly, you seem to be doing fine. You can go home as soon as the nurse brings in the paperwork."

Keira still looked confused. "Th-thanks."

Carrie spun around and caught Dylan giving her patient the thumbs up sign. She leaned in and whispered to him, "I'm not doing this for you. I'm not doing it for her or her little girl. I'm doing this because she's too damned pretty. I don't want her around here showing me up."

He chuckled, taking her arms. "For whatever reason you're doing it, thank you, Carrie."

She embraced him again and he felt her hands on his butt. "Too bad though. You were one of my most favorite conquests, Dylan." She gave him a firm squeeze and then pulled away with a sly smile.

"Thanks," he returned with a grin.

"Take care of yourself," she called over her shoulder to Keira as she left the room.

Suddenly, they were alone.

Keira sighed. "What just happened?"

He stepped forward and sat on her bed. "I called in a few cards to spring you. She'll have you out of here in no time."

She flew up, giving him an unexpected hug that made his heart race. "Oh, thank you. Thank you. I can't wait to see Delaney." She released him, but the sudden movement seemed to make her dizzy as she reached for her head again and lay back against the pillows, looking pale.

Dylan grabbed pain pills from the tray and thrust them at her with the glass of water. "Here. Take these."

"I can't. They'll—"

"Take them. I'll tell them I accidentally dropped them down the sink when I went to dispose of them for you."

"I can't let you do that. You could get into trouble."

"Take them," he insisted. "And I have one more condition for your release."

"What? A parole officer?" she quipped wryly.

"Sort of. I'm going to check in on you at home later."

She looked at him sideways.

"That's the only way this is going to happen," he insisted, his mind made up. He crossed his arms. "You need to be under medical supervision, and I'm all you've got."

She studied him for another moment and then held out her hand with a smile. "Deal."

MAX COULDN'T BELIEVE his bad luck. He'd played it so smart, too. It simply wasn't fair.

He made sure to take the license plate off his car in the mall parking lot, even though his hands froze as he wrestled with the screws. No plate, no way to identify his car. He knew it wouldn't be as easy as the first time. After all, the girl and her mother would not head for the house in the hills as Kevin did that night. Their path was fairly tame. Still, he thought he could pull it off.

And he had. Max followed her when she came out of the mall and made mincemeat of the SUV, slamming it into an unforgiving concrete garbage bin, messing up his own sedan, all to get her out of the way. The accident hadn't needed to be fatal necessarily. Max just wanted time for a thorough search of the house.

Only when he left her there bleeding and hid his car in his ailing brother's garage, and then made his way over to her little brick bungalow in his brother's car, Max found a cop posted outside. Sure, the bruiser wore no uniform, but it didn't take a genius to figure out he wasn't reading the paper he held in his hands. Max pounded the steering wheel in frustration and drove on by.

Though this was a setback, for sure, he knew a simple solution. He would just have to bide his time. Eventually he would find a way in. And, at this point, he didn't really care who got hurt in the process.

CHAPTER FIVE

Dylan pulled up in front of the address Keira had given him to find a little brick bungalow tucked into an older neighborhood near downtown Denver. He grabbed the small medical bag from the passenger's seat. It looked more like a fishing tackle box with a bright red lid and white bottom. He got out of his car, zipping up his leather jacket. He noticed a blue sedan parked across the street with a familiar face behind the wheel and waited for a pickup to pass before crossing the road.

Officer Gary Leake got out of his car and stood, leaning against it with arms crossed over his chest. He wore a Broncos coat and jeans. Dylan thought it made him look more like someone's dad than a police officer.

"What are you doing here?" the big man queried.

He shrugged. "We made a deal. I told Mrs. Kelly I'd hurry up her release, but only if she let me monitor her at home." He raised his bag as evidence.

Gary grinned, seeming strangely human. "Smooth move."

Dylan's face grew hot and he changed the subject. "You watching the house?"

The officer nodded. "Watched it last night, too. Figured whoever hit her may come back for her."

A chill ran up Dylan's spine. "You don't think it could have been random?"

"How many times have you seen someone randomly ramming someone else's car? Besides, her husband was killed in a car accident. It seems a bit too coincidental."

A glance up and down the tree-lined street revealed nothing that seemed out of character. Trash cans upside down on the curb, a lopsided snowman in a yard. Just a quiet little neighborhood. "Well, I better go see how she's doing."

"Yeah." Gary smirked.

Deciding to ignore the cop, Dylan turned and jogged across the street again, only to hear, when his tennis shoe hit the curb, a "Good luck!" shouted mockingly from behind him. He paused and shook his head but didn't turn around or respond.

He climbed the few concrete steps terracing Keira's sloped lawn and strolled down a short sidewalk to her front steps, scoping out the house as he did. The white gables hanging down above a set of windows gave it a gingerbread house feel, and wide brick steps from the front door fanned out at the bottom. At the top of the steps, a low brick wall hemmed in a small porch. Several flowerpots rested on the wall at intervals, now filled with ornaments, balls of color stacked in pyramids with greenery in between. He rang the doorbell, noting the ornate tiles with the house numbers on them, the wrought-iron hummingbird hook, which would presumably hold a hanging basket in the spring, and an old-fashioned mailbox with a flap on top. He flipped it open idly, then, withdrew his hand, feeling a little sheepish when Keira answered the door faster than expected.

She seemed much less put together than the night before, when she had been wearing snug, little jeans, and a thin ribbed, dark-grey turtle-neck sweater, accenting both her curves and eyes. Now she stood in front of him, hair pulled up into a clip in back, with strands running amuck, grey sweats and a hot-pink, over-sized pizzeria t-shirt on.

"Hi." Keira held the storm door open for him. In the natural light he could see the dark circles under her eyes that a poor night's sleep produced.

"How are you doing?" he asked, concerned.

"Not good," Keira muttered. Little feet slapped across the hardwood behind her. She smiled, though it seemed too tight in the corners, before turning. "There she is!"

Delaney ran to her and she scooped the little girl up, holding her on one hip. Today she wore a sunny pink cotton jumper over a multicolored striped turtleneck and coordinating tights. Her hair sporting two adorable pigtails, she melted against her mother, a hand curled up to her mouth. "Delaney, this is my friend...I'm sorry, I never got your name."

"Dylan. Dylan Fischer. Hi, Delaney. Nice to meet you." The little girl shrunk against her mom, but offered a smile. Keira passed through an arched opening into a living room bathed in light from the three windows across the front of the house. Dylan took in the rust-orange, Victorian, velvet couch under the windows, an ornately carved white fireplace across the room, and a few overstuffed chairs scattered here and there, covered in Chintz. A dark wood telephone stand held a large vase overflowing with fresh flowers, and a small oval carpet pulled it all together, making it cozy. It wasn't a whole lot bigger than his apartment really, but he admired her style.

"Nice place you've got here."

"Oh, thank you. It's not much, but it's big enough for me and Laney, right Lane?" She poked her daughter's tummy and the little girl giggled. "Have a seat."

Keira took one of the chairs, switching Laney to her knee, and he placed himself on the couch. On one side of the sofa an upended trunk served as an end table, with a quaint lamp on top, and in front of him another larger trunk held a wooden tray with a tea service which made the room even more inviting. Laney slipped off her mom's lap and came to stand in front of him, swinging her hips back and forth. The little girl held her hands together near her face, partially hiding behind them. She pointed to his bag. "What's in there?"

"Oh." He lifted the kit onto the table and snapped the lid open. "This is my medical bag." He turned it so she could see inside. "I'm what's called a paramedic. One of those guys who ride in an ambulance." She nodded her understanding. "I came by to see how your Mommy's doing after she got that bump on her head."

"Mommy's doing good, right, Mommy?" The little girl reached one hand back to touch Keira's knee in a protective gesture.

"Right, Lane."

Dylan peered into Keira's face and could see the strain painted in the edges as she tried to hold it together for her daughter.

"Hey, baby," she began, taking Delaney's hands in hers. "Why don't you go back and watch the rest of that TV show now."

"Okay," Delaney took off, but then turned back. "You wanna come?" she asked him.

"Maybe in a few minutes."

She accepted the answer with ease. "Okay."

After she left, the room became quiet. Keira leaned forward, her forearms on her knees, playing with a thread she had taken off Delaney's jumper.

"How are you really feeling?" Dylan asked pointedly.

She paused before answering. "Horrible." She glanced up at him, squinting in the glare of the sun.

Dylan looked down for a second, trying to hide how pleased he felt by her telling him the truth. "Did you throw up?"

She nodded, grimacing. "A couple of times." She studied the thread again, running it through her fingertips. Her fiery hair glowed redder with the light of the sun on it and he resisted the urge to smooth it down where it stuck up.

He cleared his throat. "That's to be expected," he stated, trying to sound professional. He reached out and gently took her arm. Her head flew up, but when he pressed two fingers to the inside of her wrist and checked his watch, she relaxed. Too bad he couldn't seem to do the same thing. Her soft skin about did him in. Not to mention the fact he was close enough now to smell her hair. It took him forever to find her pulse because his own pounded in his head like a bass drum. She stilled and waited for him to finish before speaking again.

"It's just...I've been trying to hide it from Laney because I don't want her to worry...but it's hard."

He nodded, looking down the hall where he could hear the sound of music he didn't recognize issuing from an open door. "Do you have any family...?"

She nodded quickly. "Yes. My sister-in-law took Delaney last night. But it's Christmas time, and she has shopping to do, and her kid's band concert is tonight..." She fluttered her hands to indicate more, but her voice trailed off.

"I understand. It's a busy time of year."

"What about you?" she interrupted, as if the thought just occurred to her. "I'm probably keeping you from work, or something."

"It's my day off," he lied. In fact, he had been forced to cash in a few more chips to cover his shift.

"Still, you probably have shopping to do."

"Actually, I'm all done. I didn't have much. Only one niece and nephew." He waved his hand in a dismissive gesture.

"Well, I really do appreciate all you've done for us—"

He cut her off. "No problem. Can I check your head now?" He pulled back one corner of the bandage on her forehead, to examine the neat row of stitches there, being as gentle as possible. "It looks good. It looks really good. But you could use a new bandage." He removed the old gauze and replaced it with a fresh bandage, and then did the same for the one on her chin. "There, that's better." He smiled at her and the corners of her lips lifted.

"Thank you."

"It's not a problem."

Laney's plaintive voice carried from the back of the house. "Are you coming, Mommy?"

"I think your mommy's going to lie down and take a nap," Dylan interjected, "but I'll come and watch with you."

"Yay!" Delaney smiley face poked around a corner comically and then disappeared again.

"I can't ask you to—"

"You didn't ask, I offered. Besides, I haven't watched any children's programs since the last time I visited my brother."

She hesitated, biting her lip in a cute way, he thought. He could feel her sizing him up. After all, he was a stranger. "I don't think I can take advantage of you." But she wavered. He could see it in her eyes.

"You're not taking advantage of me. If I went home now I'd have to clean my apartment...you're saving me from dishpan hands."

She laughed. "Well, we can't have that." She looked at him for one extra beat. "Okay, but just for a few minutes."

"Take all the time you need. I have nothing going on today." He reached into his bag and pulled out a bottle of extra-strength ibuprofen. "And take these, they'll help you sleep." He placed three into her palm. They stood in silence for a moment.

"Okay." She turned and he followed her under another archway to enter into a dining room with wainscoting on one side, and a big hutch at the far end with china in it. He didn't have time to take in details, just impressions as they passed through, crossing a hallway. He noted a door to the left which went somewhere and on the right, an open door to a bathroom, and two closed doors he guessed led to bedrooms. Next they entered a sunny, but tiny kitchen, which barely squeezed in a refrigerator and a little white wooden table with two chairs.

Keira pulled a cup out of the glass-fronted cabinets and filled it under the tap. "Can I get you something to drink?" She swallowed the pills and waited for his response.

His eyes rested on a finger-painted picture of a sunflower on a blue stem held on the refrigerator door by magnets. Above the picture, in multi-colored scrawl, he read, "Luf u Mommy and Daddy," with the "d's" backward. It seemed to fit the décor, but a brief wave of sadness washed over him. He recovered his voice. "Nah, I'm good."

"Well, if you change your mind..." She opened the fridge and bent to check its contents. He noticed her backside somehow managed to look cute even in sweats and had to quickly shift his gaze to her face when she turned around, "...there's soda, and a few beers..."

"I'll be fine, really."

Delaney appeared. "Can I have a juice box, Mommy?"

"Sure, babe." Her voice sounded tired. She grabbed one out of the door and handed it Delaney.

"Thanks," she chirped, and then she grabbed Dylan's hand, yanking him toward the doorway. "Come on."

Keira stood frozen for a second with her mouth hanging open, but then seemed to recover. "Delaney..."

Dylan, pulled off balance, stumbled into the next room, which appeared to be a playroom as toys were strewn about. A comfy old couch bordered one side, and a TV dominated the other. Keira entered behind them and hastily bent to pick up toys. He grabbed her arm.

"Leave it. It's fine."

She straightened up with a baby doll in one hand and watched as Delaney led her charge over to the couch.

He settled in. "So, what are we watching?"

"Mini-Mini Muffins."

"Ahh...Mini-Mini Muffins," he repeated wisely, but when Delaney turned he shrugged at Keira, raising both hands, palms out, and mouthed Mini-Mini Muffins with a question mark.

She chuckled, leaning against the door frame. "Are you sure about this?"

He waved her off. "Absolutely. Get some sleep."

"Okay," she returned, still sounding doubtful, but again she seemed to be struck by the sight of them momentarily. "I'll be just—" She started to gesture behind her but he interrupted.

"Delaney can show me if I need you."

"Oh, okay. I really appreciate this."

He nodded, but turned his attention to Delaney, who was tugging on his shirt and spilling forth a brief synopsis of the Mini-Mini Muffins episode about to unfold.

"Princess Pie is beautiful, isn't she?" she asked now, referring, he supposed, to the human host of the show.

"Uh-huh," he answered, although he thought Keira just as striking.

He glanced over to see that, although he felt her lingering as he spoke to Delaney, she had finally left. Dylan smiled, exhaling, glad he'd finally convinced her to let him help out.

DELANEY STOOD UP IN front of the couch, mouth hanging open, mesmerized by the action on the TV screen.

Dylan relaxed into the couch cushions and let his eyes travel around the room, coming to the conclusion it had once been a porch. The floor here consisted of some sort of cheap vinyl with alternating black and white diamonds, reminding him of a fifties diner. He had gotten a glimpse of the same flooring in the tiny bathroom between the two bedrooms, with similar black and white tile running halfway up the wall. In one corner of the playroom, he noted a monstrosity which could only be a doll house, though it faced the wall. In the opposite corner, he noticed a lot of light oozing in from under a door leading outside. He got up to check it out. Holding his hand down, he felt the cold air rushing in and thought about getting some insulation tape to fix it.

That's when his odd behavior struck him. He had come into this woman's home, a complete stranger, and offered to watch her child for her while she rested, and now he stood contemplating home improvements. What was wrong with him? Sure, the vulnerability he sensed in them and their current situation drew him in, but something more lurked underneath the surface. Delaney's sweet nature just wrapped up his heart, and Keira stirred something in his heart *and* in his blood. It wasn't just her good looks and needing someone to protect her. There was just a certain spark in her eyes, along with a soothing, open way she had about her, which he found captivating. In short, he needed to discover more about her, and the idea of exploring everything Keira thrilled him.

He wandered back to the couch, listening to Princess Pie singing about some naughty squirrels. He sank back down into the cushions when, all of a sudden, Delaney took off running. In a panic, thinking she would wake Keira, he started after her, but as soon as he rose to his feet, the little girl flew back in. She circled, and took off running again, coming back to watch the TV with such intensity he doubted she was even aware he existed anymore. After a few minutes she sped off again, only to return as before. He started to ask her what she was doing, but then he tuned into the lyrics the princess sang. "Run all you little squirrels, run," she begged. Then he got it. Delaney was acting out what the princess sang. He smiled, thinking that was about the most adorable thing he'd ever seen, and sat back down to watch her.

After some time she seemed to tucker out as she came back over to the couch and hopped up beside him. She lifted an afghan from the arm of the couch and spread it across his lap and her own, tucking it under his leg as he was sure she'd seen her mommy do before. Seconds later, the heat of her little body seeped through his jeans as she leaned into him. His put his arm around her and a contentment settled over him he hadn't felt in some time. Odd as it was, he knew this was exactly where he should be. She snuggled closer to his side, and he closed his eyes.

Geez, it's cold in here. I need to fix that gap, he thought sleepily, and nodded off.

CHAPTER SIX

A little, pointy elbow jabbed Dylan in the side and he opened his eyes. Despite the murky light the vivid blue of the TV provided, he could make out a big letter "B" and a little letter "b" apparently dancing a waltz on the screen. Delaney breathed with a steady rhythm beside him. So, they both fell asleep. He shifted a little, his body stiff, then, impulsively drew the little girl closer. She fell asleep against him. The thought warmed his heart.

He closed his eyes and tried to return to a state of slumber, but found he couldn't. Inch-by-inch, he slid his body out from beneath hers, easing Delaney down on the couch cushions as he did so. She drew her hands up to her face and burrowed deeper into the cushions. He stood gazing down at her, thinking she looked like a little cupid with rosy cheeks and lashes a deep black against pale skin. Hiis heart squeezed like he imagined it would if someone performed internal CPR on him. He reached down to stretch the blanket over her more completely. He watched her sleeping for a few seconds longer and then crept from the room, tip-toeing so as not to set off any of the creaky floorboards. He made his way to the center of the house to use the bathroom.

The bedroom door to the left of the bathroom was cracked open a few inches and he moved forward to shut it, in case Delaney woke up and started to make noise. He wanted Keira to sleep for as long as possible. But as he grasped the crystal-like doorknob in his palm, he caught sight of Keira's form on the bed and froze.

An inordinately tall bed stood in the middle of the room, constructed from golden-oak wood. It boasted acorns for the finials of the four posts, and one of those white, bumpy bedspreads with the tassels along the edges. Just the kind of bed you'd imagine for a woodland sprite. She lay facing him and he paused, feeling a sweep of sweet longing. The blankets, pulled all the way up to her chin, revealed the outline of arms crossed over chest and hands resting just under her shoulders. Her sweat pants lay in a puddle on the hardwood floor near the bed and he imagined her long, bare legs stretched out under the warmth of the covers. Her face, in repose, reminded him even more strongly of Delaney. He paused, his right hand sliding up above his head on the door frame as he leaned against it, and felt the same tug at his heartstrings. After a few seconds he reluctantly backed out of the doorway, closing the door to with a soft click.

A few minutes later, when he opened the bathroom door, Delaney waited on the other side, startling him. She smiled up, her pigtails askew.

"I'm hungry."

"You are?" he asked, pitching his voice as if surprised. He squatted down to get on her level, noting in the oven's readout over her shoulder it was almost five o'clock. She nodded, eying him with bright, hopeful eyes. "Let's see what we can find," he said with a grin.

Ten minutes later the two sat at opposite sides of the little kitchen table with matching plates of Spaghetti-Rings. Delaney insisted on sharing and even though the appearance of the noodle rings and unnaturally orange sauce did not appeal to him nearly as much as they had when he was a child, he managed to shovel in a few bites, knowing he would have heartburn later. They finished up and he washed the dishes in the sink, noticing now the lack of a dishwasher, just a strainer and mat on the counter. Delaney pulled a chair over to stand on to help dry the dishes and chatted at his side.

"Did you make that picture?" he asked during a lull in conversation. Hands stuck in sudsy water, he pointed with his elbow.

"Uh-huh," she spouted in the wise way she had. "But I was only five."

"Really?" Dylan answered appreciatively. "And how old are you now?"

"Five and three-quarters."

"I see." Spending time with her turned out to be surprisingly fun. She kept up a great conversation, covering important topics such as why it was unwise for mermaids to go on land—being part-fish—and how sharks were way scarier than lions, as someone could drown *and* be eaten by a shark at the same time.

As she finished drying the last dish, handing it to him to safely stow in the cabinet, she asked, "Wanna play?"

"Sure."

He placed his hand in her small one and let her lead him to the door opposite of Keira's. But just as they reached it, a soft knock came from the front door.

His body tensed and he listened intently for any further noise. "You go in and I'll be right back."

Closing the door behind her he crossed the front of the house, which was shrouded in darkness, trying to peer out the front window. A streetlight showed off a few trees near the curb, but the thoroughfare remained quiet, and he caught no movement on the lawn or near the house. Snow fell thick and fast while they watched TV, and he estimated several more inches of the white stuff had accumulated. He wondered about the strange silence of snow, how it could both muffle other noise, and fall without making a sound itself, so you didn't even know you were being buried beneath it.

Reaching the foyer, he searched for a switch and found it. He bathed the front stoop in light, squinting through the peep hole before pulling the door open.

Gary Leake seemed surprised, at first, to see him answering the door. He chuckled and shook his head.

Dylan scowled. "What do you need?"

"Awfully long check-up you're giving the little lady, huh?" He snickered.

"So?" he replied, crossing his arms across his chest and staring down his nose at the detective.

"Nothin'. Just an observation." The police officer studied his shoes as he swiped them across the thin layer of snow blown up to the door, appearing to fight back a smile. He lifted his head and searched the bushes on either side of the house for a second, his face becoming more serious.

"My lieutenant just told me I can't get any more overtime out here. And my wife was already plenty pissed about me staying here last night," he added, grimacing slightly. "So I gotta go. But listen—" He leaned in a little, peering at him now in earnest. "I got a feeling in here—" He pounded his wide chest. "—this guy is gonna come and try to get at this lady and her kid again. I don't know what it is. I just got this feeling."

Dylan swept his gaze across the front lawn almost without thinking but he said nothing.

"And I'm usually not wrong about these things," Leake ended ominously. "So, kid..." The smile swept back to the corner of his mouth. "You think you can hang around here for a while?" He glanced down again at his toes then added, "You know, keep an eye on things?"

Dylan thought about it. "I'll see what I can do."

The policeman laughed out loud, the sound grating on Dylan's last nerve. "You do that, son. You do that. And if you do hear anything strange, or see anything strange, you call me." He reached into his coat pocket and brought out his card, his home number already written on it in blue pen.

Dylan pocketed it. "Thanks."

Gary nodded and spun around to leave, but then turned back. "Sa-a-ay..." He drew the word out, seeming to struggle with his words, "I guess I owe you an apology for the way I acted last night."

Dylan stood staring at the policeman, recrossing his arms over his chest. The guy had been a real jerk, and he wasn't about to make it easy for him at this point.

"The wife and I, well, we've been having some troubles..." He trailed off, waving his hand vaguely. He glanced at Dylan, perhaps hoping for a little give in his stance, but receiving none. "It's just," he chuckled, shifting his feet, "sleep deprivation can be a mean thing and the couch and I, well we've become fairly well-acquainted these days, if you catch my drift."

Dylan gave a slight bob of his head.

"Well, anyways..." Leake cleared his throat. "Thanks for staying. And have a good night." He turned and started down the sidewalk, but then, as if unable to resist one last jab, he twisted back. "Don't stay up too late," he called in a sing-songy fashion, giving him a wink. Leake laughed so hard he started coughing. His chuckles floated back to Dylan, reverberating in the still night air, even as the tired policeman hit the street.

He shook his head, but chuckled. The guy was a piece of work. It was just like him to follow up an apology with something insulting. Still, Dylan sensed that under his rough exterior, Leake was really a decent human being. He stood on the doorstep several more seconds, examining the card. He watched the snow as it tried to obliterate Leake's footprints, tapping the card up and down in his palm. He glanced around one last time and then turned to latch the door behind him.

Deep in thought, he headed back to Delaney's bedroom, but when he swung the door open, he temporarily forgot about any potential danger outside. Instead, he gaped at the mural on the wall, stepping inside the room and turning in a slow circle to take it all in. In one corner, a castle dominated the scene, surrounded by a field of wildflowers, which branched off onto the other walls. A small village spread out in the opposite corner and butterflies danced about here and there. Over Delaney's bed, which hosted a blousy, white comforter and a myriad of beautifully beaded throw pillows in a mound, a Shakespearean quote spanned the wall. "To sleep, perchance to dream..." Dylan remembered his Hamlet enough to know the words were not happy ones when spoken by the Danish prince, but here they provided a lyrical effect, especially with a butterfly coming to rest on the top of the "d." Any girl would love this room, the charming whimsy of it all not even lost on him.

"Wow. This is a pretty room."

"Thank you," she answered proudly. "Mommy painted the castle and everything."

I wonder how long that took, Dylan thought with admiration.

"Want to play dolls?"

"Not exactly my choice," he mumbled with humor under his breath. But then he said out loud, "Okay."

He sat down on one of the colorful, flower throw rugs on her floor and pretended for the next half-hour, grateful a male action figure was available to him. He found it difficult to come up with appropriate comments for his doll, but Delaney, patient with the newcomer, offered suggestions whenever necessary.

"Then the bad man came in his car and crashed into them." Delaney rolled a fire truck, disproportionately larger than the sweet, red, plastic sports car the action figures sat in, ramming it into the car's side with a loud CRASH.

Dylan felt maybe he'd been playing too long when he wanted to scream out, "Not the sports car!" But he picked up on a change in Delaney's mood. She crouched, rolling the two vehicles back and forth together as if mesmerized, making more subdued crashing noises. The little girl's action figure slumped over the wheel in much the same way Keira had just the night before, only more stiffly, of course.

"Delaney?"

The little girl didn't answer, just continued to crash the cars into each other, staring at them, fixated. He reached out a hand and gently placed it on hers to still her.

When she finally looked up, he asked her, his voice soft, "That was scary, wasn't it?"

She nodded and then burst into tears. Beside himself, he scooped her up to sit with her on his knee on the side of the bed.

"Oh, honey." He brushed some loose strands of hair, damp with tears, out of her face. "It's okay, now. You and your mommy are fine and nothing like that is ever going to happen again." *Not if I can help it,* he vowed on impulse. He hugged her close to his chest and rocked back and forth, searching for more comforting words, but then the door swung open, and Keira entered.

In a flash Delaney hopped off his lap and ran to her. "Mommy. Mommy! You're up." She gave her mom a sunny smile, the tears hardly dry on her face.

Dylan, however, did not recover as quickly. He didn't even meet Keira's eyes fully as he mulled over Delaney's actions, recognizing how frightened she still must be.

"Hey, Lane." Keira hugged her to her knees but watched him with bright eyes. After a beat she asked Delaney if she could go get a hairbrush and she scampered off leaving the two of them alone. "I'm so sorry. It's much later than I intended. I must have set the alarm wrong."

"Hmm...oh, no, that's okay."

"It's dark outside. It must be nearly five."

"Six, I think," he mumbled absentmindedly. Delaney returned, hairbrush in hand. He glanced over at Keira's somewhat rumpled form and decided she looked cute. *Still and all,* he thought, *I wish she had just left the sweatpants off because I would like to see those long legs underneath the hem of her t-shirt.*

"Well...I'm not sure if you have time, but I'd like to make it up to you. Can I cook dinner for you or something? You must be starving." She stared off into the corner of the room, placing a hand under her chin. "I could make something quick...like spaghetti..." Delaney was about to open her mouth, but Dylan, realizing she intended to tell Keira they'd already eaten, caught her attention and shook his head in an exaggerated fashion, putting a finger to his lips. She smiled confidentially and put her own little finger to her lips, too, giggling.

"That would be great," he told Keira before she could catch on.

"It would?" she responded, her eyebrows raising. "You want to have dinner with us?" Her face brightened for the first time and again he caught a glimpse of Delaney there.

"I'd love to."

Delaney laughed and ran over to hug Dylan's leg.

"What's with you, silly girl?" Keira ruffled Delaney's hair as she passed her on the way back out of the room. "You're awfully giggly all of a sudden."

As Keira headed toward the kitchen, he gave Delaney a wink and swung her up over his shoulder to peals of laughter.

CHAPTER SEVEN

Keira began rooting through the refrigerator, hoping to find all of the ingredients she needed to make a decent dinner. She could hear Dylan and Delaney behind her, whooping it up, which warmed her heart. Delaney, always one of those kids who took a little while to warm up to people, had been especially reticent with men since Kevin's death. Whatever Dylan was doing with her, it worked.

Then she took a second to acknowledge it worked for her, too. He evoked sensations she hadn't felt since she and Kevin first started dating, and...it was all right. She hadn't thought it could be all right to have thoughts like this about anybody other than Kevin, but if she found the man attractive, what was the harm? She'd hardly be a woman if she didn't swoon a little when she saw those bulging biceps swinging her little girl up over his shoulder. It was perfectly natural.

She chuckled under her breath, grabbed some Italian sausage out, and closed the fridge. Obviously the nap had done her some good. Dylan searched around and came up with a frying pan, moving about her as if involved in a synchronized swimming routine in the tiny kitchen.

She retrieved a jar of spaghetti sauce from the cupboard and thought about what she heard when she woke up. She remembered opening her eyes slowly and for the first time since the accident—if you could call it that, it seemed pretty purposeful, she had to admit—a headache didn't rage. She moved her head with the utmost caution to peer in the direction of the door and didn't feel her eyeballs roll around in her head, unable to catch up to the rest of her, like she had been feeling. Not to mention, the door was both in focus, and not spinning.

When she got dressed and reached Delaney's door, she could hear Dylan's gentle voice.

"That was scary, wasn't it?"

Her heart clutched in her throat when Delaney burst into tears. She reached for the doorknob, but paused again when he comforted her. "Oh, honey. It's okay, now. You and your mommy are fine and nothing like that is ever going to happen again." She gripped the handle until her knuckles hurt and squeezed her eyes shut, fighting back tears. As much as Delaney needed to hear those reassuring words, it helped Keira to hear it, too. "It's okay," he said. For awhile now she had wondered if it could ever be okay without Kevin.

When she opened the door and saw Delaney in Dylan's arms, emotion swamped her again.

Now, as she stood over the sink, peeling an onion she found in the fridge for the sauce, she marveled at how natural it all felt, despite Dylan being a virtual stranger to them. She slid her eyes in his direction. He was opening the jar of spaghetti sauce for her. His jeans fit him...oh, so well, and his arms showed the muscles which came with lifting people every day. He wore a short-sleeved navy t-shirt with a firehouse logo on it, which kind of added to his sexiness, as far as she was concerned. He was more filled in than Kevin, with broader shoulders. She could tell his short brown hair would have a little curl to it if allowed to grow out.

She lowered her eyes and pretended to be concentrating on her onion when he came over to wash his hands in the sink next to her. His arm grazed hers and something stirred in her, a quickening of her heartbeat she hadn't felt in a long time.

He leaned on the sink, both hands gripping the edge. "So how are you feeling?"

She cleared her throat before lifting her gaze to answer him. "A whole lot better."

"Good."

She liked the easy way he grinned at her. She put the onion down and started slicing radishes for the salad.

"Now..." He gave her a nudge. "What do you want me to do?"

"Nothing. I've got this. You just go and relax. Do you want a beer?"

"Sure. I'll get it." He fished one out of the fridge, left over after a weekend during the summer when her brother-in-law had helped her to fix a running toilet. After popping the cap, he walked over and dropped it into the trash. As he leaned back against the counter, he caught her eye. "So you did the mural in Delaney's room?"

"Yes," she smiled, but her face flushed. Delaney had disappeared somewhere, leaving them alone. Nervousness stole over her.

"That's pretty impressive. How long did it take you?"

"Umm—" She avoided his eyes. "—it took a while. We had just moved here, and...I wasn't back to work yet..."

In her grief, it had become a sort of unhealthy obsession for her. She'd become preoccupied with making the best room possible, deciding—illogically—that it was the only thing she could do to help Delaney get over the loss of her father. She'd painted well into the night, while Delaney slept on the couch or in her big bed. Her hands had shaken, eyes had gone bleary with tears, as she worked herself ragged. The morning she woke up slumped over a can of paint, with a crease on her forehead from resting it on the can's lid, she had decided she needed to go back to school and reestablish some normalcy in their lives.

Keira felt Dylan studying her. She changed the subject. "So, you've been a paramedic for a while?"

"Two years." He took a pull on his beer. "Before that I was a rep for a pharmaceutical company. I made a lot of money, but it wasn't exactly giving me a rush every morning, if you know what I mean."

"Mmm-hmm." She nodded. Newly widowed, one of the things which really pulled her out of her funk was the fact she loved her job as a teacher.

"Can I chop the onion for you?" he offered.

"Sure." She handed it to him and their fingertips touched. She looked away, chastising herself for being so stupid. She was acting like the shy eighteen-year-old she'd been when she first met Kevin. "Uhh...I'll get you a knife." She began to reach for the knife block.

"Already got one," Dylan replied, brandishing his blade with a grin.

"Oh, okay. The cutting board is—"

"In the corner." He retrieved it and started cutting in silence, giving her a chance to catch her breath.

She started browning the sausage, got a pan of water going for the noodles, and clicked the oven on to preheat for garlic bread. She searched for something to say. "So, how did you like Mini-Mini Muffins?"

"It was...different," he commented. "But, I have to admit, we dozed off for a while."

She reached in the refrigerator for a bag of lettuce. *We? So he means both he and Delaney.* The image froze her for a second and she turned to gaze at him, but he chopped away at the onion, apparently oblivious. A small smile tugged at her lips as she closed the fridge. Stretching up on her toes, Keira could just reach the cabinet above the fridge where she kept the big bowl for the salad. She could just graze it with her fingertips and she managed to spin it repeatedly as she tried to get it to wobble over within her reach.

"I'll help you."

The bowl spun too close to the edge and teetered dangerously. She threw her hands in position to protect her head but Dylan appeared in a flash. They both juggled the bowl for a second or two, but he gained control of it. She spun, practically wedged against the refrigerator by his body. Their faces were inches away from each other. Her heart galloped in her chest, making it hard to speak.

"Th-that was stupid of me," she stammered, pushing a strand of hair behind her ear to try to calm herself.

He stood motionless, staring down into her face, still holding the bowl above her head. She felt a sense of panic. She needed to get away from this man. His masculine scent filled her nostrils and the heat from his body warmed her.

"Thank you," she prompted, hoping he would move.

"Hmm?" he murmured in a dazed sort of way. "Oh." He stepped back, practically shoving the bowl into her hands. "Here." He returned to his cutting board.

Without warning Delaney tore into the room. "Mommy. Mommy! It's snowing!" She pulled on Keira's arm dragging her into the front room.

Keira laughed. "You'd think it hadn't snowed eighteen out of the last twenty days."

Dylan wiped his hands on a kitchen towel and followed behind.

She climbed up on the couch with Delaney, kneeling and resting her hands on the back of the couch as she did, staring out the big picture window. "Wow. It's really coming down out there. We've already gotten a few inches. I hope you won't have any trouble getting home."

"Nah," he responded, dismissing the idea. "I think they said it would stop by seven."

"Hmm." She watched the snow falling like a curtain in front of the window for a second, then stirred, scrambling down from the couch. "Okay, baby girl, how 'bout we go finish the spaghetti so we can have dinner."

Delaney hopped down and rushed back off to the TV room, calling over her shoulder. "I'm not hungry."

"Not hungry?" she wondered out loud. "I thought she'd be starved by now."

Dylan shrugged. "Kids."

"Yeah. That's for sure." She passed him and headed back to the kitchen. When he didn't follow, she turned back. He stepped up to the window and scoped the lawn from left to right. Could he actually be more worried about the snow than he was letting on?

He turned, and seeing her watching him, started. "Ooh. I'm coming."

When they got back to the kitchen, she popped the bread in the oven, drained the sausage and added the sauce. Then she threw the noodles into the water. He brushed past her on the way to adding the onions to the sauce. She dumped the salad into the bowl and stepped on the pedal to open the little stainless steel trash can and throw the bag away. An open can of Spaghetti-Rings balanced on top of the garbage. She swiveled her head and caught sight of the two spoons in the strainer which hadn't been there before.

When he turned around she held the Spaghetti-Ring's can up accusingly. "What's this?"

"Uh. Laney was hungry and I... made...some...Spaghetti-Ring's," he ended, sounding defeated.

She laughed. "Are you even hungry?"

"Yes. I swear. They sort of...well...sucked, to be truthful."

"Okay," she returned doubtfully. She picked up a wooden spoon to stir the sauce with and waved it at him. "But you better eat every bite of my spaghetti."

"I will. I promise."

"Hmphf," she snorted, but she smiled to herself as she stirred the sauce. She had forgotten how much she missed adult company.

"What else can I do?"

"Umm...you could set the table, I guess. I planned on eating in the dining room," she teased, "but since it's only the two of us, I suppose we can eat in here." She turned to smile at him over her shoulder.

"You got it."

"The placemats—" She raised an eyebrow. "Or do you know where those are, too?"

Dylan laughed. "No."

Her lips curled up slightly. "In the hutch in the dining room. Top drawer."

Minutes later, Keira ladled steaming hot spaghetti onto two plates, but as she turned around to set them on the table she paused. Dylan had swiped a candle from the dining room table. She lifted her gaze to his with a question mark in them.

He shifted, looking sheepish. "Uh, ambiance?"

She set the plates down without saying anything, but couldn't hide her smirk. When they sat down, their knees almost touched under the table.

They chit-chatted about nothing important for a while. Keira told Dylan a few funny stories about her kindergarten class and found him a good listener with a sense of humor similar to her own. When he finished his salad and moved on to the spaghetti he commented, "This is good."

"Better than your Chef Luigi's with Laney?" she countered teasingly.

"Oh, no. Chef Luigi's rules. It was Spaghetti-Rings with Delaney, a pale comparison to the Chef."

"Is it now? So 'the Chef's' is better than mine?"

"Hell, yeah!"

"Well!" She slammed her napkin down on the table and began to rise.

He grabbed her wrist. "I'm just kidding. Yours is delicious," he said seriously, his eyes turning a softer shade of green.

She had been playing with him at first, but at the touch of his hand, her system went into overdrive. That, combined with the look she saw in his eyes, put her in an acute state of panic. She snatched her arm away and rubbed it as if he left a mark on her. She knew she was overreacting and turned away from him to hide her feelings.

"Keira, I..."

It was imperative for her to stop him from speaking any further. She tried to regain her playful mood, but her words came out shaky. "No, it's too late. You already chose Chef Luigi over me."

He couldn't seem to respond at first. "Oh, come on," he returned after several seconds, "he is *so* not my type. The cheesy mustache and floppy hat..."

She laughed. "Just for that, you're doing the dishes."

"Fine. It's a fair punishment."

She sat back down and they continued on with light banter while they finished up dinner, lingering at the table as they found out more about each other. She opened a bottle of wine for Dylan but both thought it unwise for her to have even one glass. He leaned back in his chair as he told her about growing up the youngest of three boys in the little mining town of Silverton, Colorado.

"My mom passed away in a boating accident my junior year of high school, so it was just my dad and me. Keith and Tom were away at school. My dad and I were always close, but during that time we became constant companions. We fished every weekend, and, whenever I didn't have homework, during the week. We never went out on the boat, though, after Mom's accident." He stopped talking, staring at his wine glass as he twirled it around by the stem on the table.

She placed her hand on his arm. "I know how difficult it is to lose someone you love." The words were hard to say, but she needed to say them somehow.

He covered her hand with his, rubbing his thumb over it thoughtfully. "Yeah. Losing Mom was devastating, but losing my dad a few years later was worse. When Mom died, I concentrated on helping Dad. When he died, I threw myself into being a paramedic." He leaned forward. "Somewhere along the way, I seemed to have lost myself, and I guess I'm just starting to realize that."

Hadn't she done the same thing? Throwing herself into being a mother to Delaney?

He released her hand and stood suddenly, taking the plates to the sink. "I've been talking your ear off. Tell me more about you."

Keira touched on marrying her high school sweetheart, getting pregnant unexpectedly in their first months of marriage, and finishing up her degree by attending night school. She could feel Dylan observing her at times as they cleaned up the kitchen. With the last pot put away, it seemed like an appropriate time to thank him and say goodnight, but she wasn't ready for him to leave yet.

"It's awfully quiet. I wonder what Laney's up to." She walked around the wall into the TV room and he followed. Delaney lay fast asleep on the couch, a stuffed dog and cat hugged to her chest. "Oh," Keira cooed. "I better get her in bed." She moved to pick her up, but he touched her arm.

"Let me," he whispered. She nodded and stepped back.

Dylan carefully scooped up his earlier playmate and carried her toward the bedrooms. Keira went ahead of him and opened the door, turning down the sheet. Keeping the child close to his body, he eased her down into her bed. Keira pulled up the covers and they stood back for a second, watching her. Then she reached up to switch off the little chandelier lamp. As they snuck off toward the light from the kitchen flowing in through the open door, Keira reached out to take Dylan's hand, telling herself it was only to help make her way in the dark.

When she softly shut the door behind her, she leaned against it, hands behind her back still clutching the knob.

"Thank you for everything." She sighed with a smile.

To her amazement he reached out and touched her hair, running his hand down to her shoulder and leaving it there. She could hardly breathe. His eyes traveled between hers and it seemed almost as if he held his breath, too.

"I guess I should go," he murmured hesitantly.

She found she could say nothing. He lifted his hand from her shoulder and dropped it to his side and something inside her cried out.

They ambled to the front room, not bothering to turn on any lights. It was fairly well-lit from the outdoor streetlights. She glanced at his face and could tell he was thinking hard about something. All of a sudden the wind howled like only the wind in the Rockies could. His head snapped up, searching the room and the lawn beyond the windows.

"It's only the wind," she reassured him.

He looked at her, and again outside. "It's really coming down."

She followed his gaze. "Yeah. You're right."

He paused and seemed to be thinking of something to say.

"I wish I'd gotten those new tires on my car. I'd hate to get stuck out tonight." He looked at her.

She hesitated. "Well, I'd hate for you to go out if you think you might have trouble."

He dropped his gaze for a second. "Do you think I could...sleep on your couch tonight? I won't try anything, I'll stay out here all night and go home first thing in the morning," he added quickly.

She almost had to laugh at how adamantly he proclaimed the innocence of his intentions. "I'll go get you some blankets."

CHAPTER EIGHT

Dylan stared out at the night. Nothing unusual, except for this nagging feeling inside of him he was doing something wrong.

When Keira came back with a stack of blankets, he patted the couch beside him, his brow furrowed, asking her to sit down. "Keira, I don't want to start things off by lying to you," he said carefully. "There's nothing wrong with my car, other than it's a piece of crap, that is. But...the tires are the newest thing on it, and I wasn't really concerned about the weather."

"Okay," she responded, sounding confused, but smiling.

He looked down at the space between them, trying to formulate the right words. He didn't like lying to her, but he didn't want to frighten her either. He didn't want to add any more to what she already dealt with in recovering from the accident. After a while he decided shooting straight was, after all, probably the best solution. "There's been a police officer outside of your home watching the house. He's afraid whoever hit you the other night may mean you further harm. But the policeman had to leave, and that's why I wanted to stay—" He glanced around. "—to watch over things."

Keira sat very still. He tried to read her face as she absorbed the information, but he didn't know her well enough to gage her emotions. After a few moments, she stood up, but didn't speak at first. She fidgeted with her fingers. "But you're a paramedic, not a cop."

He nodded, not sure where she was going.

She began collecting the blankets. "Dylan, you need to leave."

"Huh?"

She dropped a sheet and bent to snatch it up, her jaw tight.

He could tell he'd upset her. He grabbed her arm before she could turn away from him. "Wait—"

"You don't belong here!" she practically shouted at him, and, even in the dim light, he could see anger on her face and fear.

"I want to—" he began, searching for an explanation.

"No!" Then, probably afraid she might wake Laney, she dropped her voice. "Listen—" Her eyes flashed and Dylan wished more than anything he could take back whatever he had done to hurt her. "You don't have to feel some...some...obligation... to take care of me. You stopped on the road and helped me when I was hurt and I'm grateful. You don't have to continue to..." She seemed at a loss for words. He held her shoulders, waiting for an explanation. "Laney and I are fine here. I can take care of us." She seemed to forget the volume level again.

"I know." Now he felt confused.

She took a deep breath, and he could feel the tension drain out of her shoulders. "You don't have to worry about us." She dropped her head. "Or feel sorry for us." Her voice sounded small.

"Keira, I—"

Again she seemed to gather herself, running her top hand over the pile of blankets as if to straighten out any wrinkles. He marveled at the swing her emotions took in such a short period of time. "You did your job patching me up, but that's where it ends. You're not a cop. You aren't paid to tangle with the criminal element." She looked him straight in the eye. "You can go home now. You've done your duty. I appreciate it."

He wasn't sure what he had said or done to make her angry, he just knew he wanted to take it all back. As she turned to storm away from him, his own anger sparked. He again reached for her elbow before she could get away from him.

"Now, wait just one minute."

She looked at him with those incredible grey eyes which now spat fire at him, and he couldn't find the words to say to her. "What did I do to make you angry?" he blurted out.

"N-nothing. You did nothing," she stammered. "I'm sorry. I guess—" She tossed the pile of blankets back onto the couch and began pacing, running her hand through her hair. "I guess I must just be tired, from the accident."

He moved in front of her as she turned to pace away, marveling at his own boldness and the surge of his emotions. He barely knew her. "Bullshit. Don't use that cop out. Tell me why you're mad."

"I'm not...mad, exactly. I'm..." She studied her fingers. "It's just..." She tilted her head to one side as if concentrating. "I thought you stayed..." She trailed off, and then her gaze flicked up. She let out a frustrated huff. "I thought," she annunciated distinctly, "we were having a good time. I thought you stayed because you wanted to, not because you felt like you had to." She stomped over and flopped down on the couch. "I feel like an idiot."

He smiled. So someone else was having trouble dealing with their emotions besides him. "There's no need to—" he started.

"Oh, shut up." Keira grabbed one of the throw pillows off of the couch and hugged it to her middle. She scowled at no one in particular.

He came and sat down next to her, saying nothing for several seconds to let her settle. He sighed, putting a hand on her knee. "Yes, I promised Officer Leake I'd keep an eye on you. But before I even talked to him I was trying to figure out a way to stick around a while longer. Keira," he bent his head to catch her gaze and draw her head up, "from the moment Delaney sat on my lap, she had me wrapped around her finger. And from the moment I saw you, hurt, behind the wheel of your car—shit, from the moment I found you in the crowd at the mall, you've been on my mind like a bad song." His own honesty surprised him.

"That doesn't sound pleasant." She took a deep breath and her eyes made the tell-tale trip from his eyes to his lips and back again in an instant.

His voice changed, became softer. The streetlight lit her face and he was captivated by her. He ran a hand down her cheek. "I went to the hospital, I came to your house, because I wanted to find out more about you."

A small smile haunted her mouth, but then she asked with a nervous hitch in her voice, "And?"

He wondered why a beautiful girl like her needed so much reassurance. "I found out you have one hell of a temper," he teased.

"Oh!" she exclaimed, batting him with the pillow.

"Somebody's feeling better." He took the pillow from her and winged it onto an armchair without even looking. Then he gave into the urge he had been fighting all night and grabbed her, pulling her close. "And I found out it's hard to be around you and not kiss you." He leaned in, brushing his lips over hers, savoring the moment. The sound of her breath quickening drove him over the edge. He covered her lips with his, closing his eyes and losing himself to the kiss, diving in, tasting her, and liking what he found. It took all of his willpower to pull back to see if she approved, and when he did, the desire he saw matched in her eyes fueled him more. He released his hold on her waist, brought his hands to either side of her face, feeling her silky hair slide over his knuckles, because he wanted to take control of this next kiss.

He brushed a thumb over her lips in anticipation and then angled his mouth again to hers, feeling a sudden desperateness rise inside of him. Usually it took a little bit of time and encouragement to turn him into an animal, but she did something to him no other woman had before. Like a shot of adrenaline to his heart, his body became hard with passion, and desire darkened his vision.

She shifted, her mouth warm, body pressing against his, that soft, tempting body. He felt the curves of her breasts under the t-shirt, smelt her perfume, and thought he just might lose it altogether. But then she pulled back.

"Wait," She panted, gazing at him with a wild expression. "I feel dizzy."

He immediately became concerned, not to mention swamped with guilt. "You do?" He should have never pressed her when she'd just gotten out of the hospital less than twenty-four hours ago. "Any blurry vision?"

She laughed. "Not from that."

His attitude changed from worried to cocky in an instant. He gave her a shit-eating grin. "I do sometimes have that effect on women."

She swatted him on the shoulder.

"Ouch! You're violent." He slipped his arm around her and pulled her back into the couch cushions. "I guess I should take it easy on you." He rubbed her arm, happy just to sit with her.

She pulled her legs up, curling them under her and leaning into his embrace. They sat in silence as the snow continued to blow just outside the glass behind them.

"I should make you go," she murmured.

"Not a chance." He trailed his fingers up and down her arm. Finally, he sighed. "You should get some sleep."

She didn't move at first, but then sat up, her eyes searching his. "If you hear *anything*, you'll call 9-1-1. Promise me you won't try to be the hero."

He crossed his heart, then, replied in a serious tone, "I'm no dummy, Keira." He pulled her in again and kissed her forehead near the bandage tenderly.

"And you'll be here in the morning?"

"I'll be here in the morning."

"Good night, then." Before he could think, she kissed him softly, with just a hint of sweet temptation, the kind of kiss that lingered on the lips long after it ended, and then she disappeared into the darkness of the next room.

After he fixed his "bed," he walked around the house, checking the locks, stopping outside her bedroom for a minute and thinking about the kiss. He watched it snow for a while, pulled the filmy curtain across the picture windows behind the couch after checking for footprints in the snow, and then he laid down. He thought about Keira and what he liked about her. He liked the guts he saw in her, raising a kid alone, going on after losing her high school sweetheart. He liked her sense of humor and feistiness. He liked the depth of emotion he sensed in her, and the easy way she was with Delaney. And he liked, he really, really liked, the heart-stopping way she kissed him. With that thought in mind, and the idea someone could be after her, he tossed and turned all night. He got up several times and checked the house, but always returned to his little nest on the couch to think and dream about her some more.

MAX PARKED HIS WIFE's car in a back alley. As he watched from behind some trees along the far side of the driveway, he saw the policeman leave his car and approach the house. Peeking out from his hiding place, he wasn't able to make out who the cop was talking to at first, but the male voice responding to the cop's got his attention. He took a chance and moved closer to the street to get a better angle and was surprised to see the paramedic at her door. What the heck? He wasn't able to make out their conversation, much to his frustration. He only knew the cop left, but the paramedic didn't.

He watched as the paramedic scanned the lawn, eyes never nearing his hiding place, and then he turned and went back inside, closing the door behind him. The cop left in his blue car, and Max waited for the paramedic to take his leave. Hours later, as he stamped his feet and breathed on his hands in the cold, he began to wonder if the paramedic planned to leave at all.

After a time, he decided it didn't matter. He needed to get into the house, paramedic or no paramedic.

CHAPTER NINE

Keira couldn't sleep. Had she really kissed the cute paramedic? And how did she feel about that? Well, there was a reason she couldn't sleep. The reason was, she really kissed the cute paramedic, and she wasn't at all sure how she felt about that. Her body told her one thing; it was sensational. Her mind, well that was another story. Kevin hadn't even been gone a year. For someone she'd promised to love all her life, that wasn't very long. On the other hand, the past eleven months seemed like a lifetime for her, and maybe it was time to move on, make some changes in her life.

She thought about the kiss, and flopped onto her side, grabbing the pillow from the empty side of the bed and squeezing it in frustration. In one day she had gone from not knowing Dylan outside of a Santa costume, to being lip-locked with him on her couch. It made her want to squeal, and it made her want to cry. She didn't even know this man. He could be some twisted Santa serial killer, or he could be a really sweet, *really* sexy paramedic who seemed to be a great guy. *Ugh!* Her mind reeled. Maybe, by some weird twist, he was the man who ran her off the road. No, she told herself. He couldn't be. She saw the man, and it wasn't Dylan. What was happening to her?

She just needed to get some sleep. She flopped on her back, trying to make heads or tails of her reflection in the brass ceiling fan fixture in the dark and thinking of the hot man lying just yards away on the couch which her mom once owned. Maybe she was cracking up. Maybe no one ran her off the road, maybe she imagined it all and she just wrecked the vehicle herself. No. People had witnessed it.

She twisted onto her stomach. She could never sleep in this position, but sometimes it felt good and could get her tired enough so she could turn on her back and fall asleep. But not tonight. Tonight all she could think about was Dylan Fischer.

And what about this idea that someone might be lurking outside who wanted her dead? And why? Why would anyone want her dead? She wasn't foolish enough to think she'd never annoyed anyone or gotten on their nerves. But make someone mad enough to want to kill her? And if he did come back, what would Dylan be able to do against a guy crazy enough to ram his vehicle into hers over and over again?

With a sudden thought, she hopped out of bed and lay flat on the floor in her t-shirt, reaching with her left hand under the bed. It had to be there somewhere. Her fingers hit upon a smooth cylindrical shape. The wooden bat rolled to her noisily and she smiled in triumph. Kevin had always kept the bat under their bed in case of intruders. She tiptoed across her bedroom floor, forgetting, in her haste, to put sweatpants back on. She creaked open the door and crept out. She took a few steps toward the living room, but froze at a noise behind her.

Someone was in her house. Her heart pounding, she turned and swung with all her might.

She saw a figure duck as the bat sliced through the air. The bat was snatched out of her hand.

"Holy shit, Keira! You about took my head off."

"Dylan!" she screamed, her heart still racing. She impulsively jumped into his arms. To her surprise, he lifted her off the ground and slid the hand with the bat under her rear, tromping with her toward the living room. She wrapped her legs around his trunk and laid her head down on his shoulder. "Oh, my gosh. You scared me."

"Well—" He grunted. "You scared me, too." He set her down by the couch and dropped the bat on it, letting it roll to the back as he sat, legs spread apart, and ran a hand through his thick hair. "Geez. Let me get my heartrate back to normal." He glanced up at her finally. "Are you okay?" She nodded. "My God, what were you doing?"

"I brought the bat out here so you could protect yourself."

"From what? You?"

She began to giggle, taking in his mussed hair and hearing the somewhat comic exasperation in his voice. She tried to cool it so her apology would come out sincerely. "I'm sorry."

He began to laugh at himself, too. "Well, you should be."

She noticed for the first time he didn't have a shirt on, and even in what little light came through the window she could make out a muscled chest and arms she was entirely unworthy of, but willing to accept. "I'll make it up to you," she purred, stepping over to stand in front of him.

"How?" he asked, suspicion coloring his voice. But his hands already came up to touch the bare skin of the back of her thighs. Her body responded, her butt muscles clenched, her stomach became tight, and mini-sirens sounded everywhere. His hands, strong and sure as they cruised upward, cupped her rear and pulled her pelvis toward him. "How are you going to make it up to me, Keira?" he questioned her, his voice a silky challenge.

Boldly she smoothed her hands over his bare shoulders and back up, sucking in her breath a little when she felt the definition beneath her fingertips. Then she slid them down in front of his shoulders and gave him a shove backward. With racy deliberateness she brought one knee up onto the couch by his side, and then the other, straddling him. He watched her in the dark, and she didn't need to see him clearly to tell she had totally turned him on. She raked the tips of her long nails along the stubble of his cheeks, the noise it made as sharp and edgy as she felt, and tilted his head up.

"Like this," she replied, and then lowered her lips to his, drawing him into a long and sensual kiss which sent them both humming.

When she pulled away he choked out, "You're forgiven."

She laughed, relishing the power she felt. "Good night, Dylan." She started to climb off his lap, but only got one foot on the floor before he grabbed her by the waist and twisted to throw her down on the mound of couch pillows.

"You're not going anywhere yet," he growled, and then he crushed his lips to hers. Where he received what she offered before, now he took what he wanted.

Keira was going under. His hands slid up, firm, underneath her t-shirt, scrunching it up as he went, to just beneath her breasts. His thumbs rubbed the super-soft skin there, but he ventured no further, driving her mad. He moved his mouth lower to nibble on her chin, to the left of her bandage and then, as she arched, his lips swept along her throat as she let out a low moan.

A voice inside her head kept telling her she needed to stop, her daughter slept in the next room, but she kept hoping the voice would drown in the swirl of sensations he was creating. "Dylan." She exhaled, hearing the sound of her own need in his name. Again the inner voice raged. She couldn't do this. She'd just met him for God's sake. Then his teeth bit into her shoulder and a moan escaped her lips.

He buried his head in her hair. "Keira." The sound of his husky voice near her ear aroused her even further. A primal need arose within and her fingers clutched at his back, the nails digging into his flesh.

"Mmm," was the only sound she could manage.

"If your daughter wasn't in the next room, I might have a hard time stopping." He sighed.

She stilled.

He took some of his weight off her and leaned against the back of the couch. "Tell me there'll be a time when I won't have to stop," he begged. "Please, Keira. Promise me."

Keira traced his lips with one finger, feeling sad and disappointed. She couldn't find her voice.

He dropped his gaze. "I shouldn't have asked for that. I'm sorry. We hardly know each other and—"

She pressed one finger to his lips to make him stop talking. "I promise, Dylan," she murmured, though incredulous she spoke the words at all. Then he did the sweetest thing ever. He took her hand and brought it to his lips to kiss. She melted.

He stood clumsily and held out his hands to help her up. "Good night."

She gave him a soft, quick kiss.

She turned to walk away but he grabbed her shoulders and pulled her roughly back against him. He slipped his arms around her and squeezed tight whispering in her ear, "You drive me crazy, you know."

She smiled, turning her head slightly to see him. "Yes, I know." She giggled and he pushed her off, slapping her rear as she left.

She sighed, wishing she could just lie down beside him and snuggle up on the couch. She entered the bedroom and shut the door behind her.

CHAPTER TEN

When Dylan woke up, the tempting smell of cinnamon rolls floated in from the kitchen. He stretched but kept his eyes shut, choosing to relive the evening with Keira rather than get up. Uum, but the girl was hot. Way hot. When the gorgeous redhead had straddled him, something had exploded inside of his head. Usually he liked to take things slow and be deliberate in his actions with women, savoring each stage of the relationship, and always keeping them wanting for more. He didn't know what was wrong this time around. It seemed like she awoke some animal inside. With her kiss, her touch, he wanted nothing more but to be inside her, tangled up together so intricately no one could tell where one ended and one began. It was insane. He had never felt anything like it before.

"Why are you hugging the baseball bat?"

The little voice came from so close that he nearly flew out of his skin. "Delaney!"

"Hi, Dylan."

He reached out a hand and pulled her up to the side of the couch, an arm folded behind her knees. "How did you sleep?" he asked with a smile.

"Good," Delaney responded cheerily. "I didn't know you and Mommy were having a sleepover."

Dylan wanted to chuckle. He'd just love to have a "sleepover" with Keira. At the same time, panic hit. How should he respond? He drew out his answer, thinking about the words with care. "Well, I just stayed because of the bad weather and your mom was nice enough to let me sleep on the couch."

Without warning, Delaney crawled on top of his stomach, forcing air out of his lungs and coming perilously close to creating some other very unpleasant sensations for him. She stared out the window.

"It doesn't look so bad to me."

Keira chose that most perfect of times to enter from the kitchen. She wore dark jeans tucked into a pair of black, knee-high boots, hugging her calves sensually, and a white sweater with a wide, black belt. She looked better than the cinnamon rolls smelt, which was saying something. She held a spatula casually in one hand.

"Oh, sorry. Delaney, get off Mr. Fischer, please. The poor man just woke up."

Dylan rolled, snatching Delaney and then setting her down in his lap to tickle her for a second or two before allowing her release. Delaney made good on her escape, racing from the room. Once alone, he offered a smile. "Good morning." He grabbed his t-shirt and pulled it on, then stood up, buttoning his jeans. "Did you make cinnamon rolls? They smell wonderful."

"Oh. They are just the kind you pop open on the counter," she answered with a dismissive wave of the hand.

"I haven't even eaten those in a while."

The corners of her lips turned up a trifle. "Man, are you easy to please. Well, you better get your cute little buns in the kitchen before they're all gone. Delaney would demolish the whole batch if left unattended."

With a grin, he followed the sexy redhead into the kitchen. Noting Delaney was distracted with unraveling her cinnamon roll before eating it, he saw his chance to sneak up behind Keira.

"You think my buns are cute, eh?"

She shrugged, playing hard to get. "Maybe."

"But you said—"

She spun away but smiled over her shoulder at him with a twinkle in her eyes. "Laney, finish up your milk or we're going to be late for school."

"Is Dylan going to school, too?"

"I don't know. Are you going to school, Dylan?" Keira teased.

"No. Definitely not." He squatted down by Delaney's chair. "I've got to go back to my work as a paramedic today."

"Okay," she responded, nonplussed, hopping down from her chair and running off.

He remained motionless, his mouth hanging open for a second. "Glad to see she's all choked up about it," he grumbled.

Keira smothered a giggle. "I'm sure she's hurting deep down on the inside, where it counts."

"Whatever," he replied, pretending to storm off, but she grabbed him by the waist and pulled him to her.

"I'll miss you today," she whispered in his ear, checking to see if Delaney was still out of sight.

"Will you?" He turned around and pushed her hair back to tug on her bandage a little. "Can I check this?"

"I think you already are."

He ignored her remark. "Looks good. Looks really good. Do you want me to replace this bulky bandage with a couple of Band-Aids?"

She pretended to be thoughtful. "I think I'd garner more sympathy with a bigger bandage."

"Okay. If that's what you want." He started to move away, but she pulled him back again.

"A Band-Aid would be nice," she answered contritely. Her gaze shifted to somewhere over his shoulder and she quickly released him.

"Hey, what's going on?" Delaney had just returned to the kitchen with her backpack.

"Mr. Fischer was just checking my bandage for me."

Delaney peered at her mom, suspicion arching her eyebrows, with hands on hips. "Then why were you holding him?"

Dylan's head swiveled from one to the other. It was like watching a segment of "Point/Counterpoint." He held his breath in anticipation of Keira's next move.

"So I could keep still while he examined my cut, missy," she returned sternly, seeming unaware of having adapted the same stance by placing hands on her hips.

Good move, he thought. Just pull out the adult authority card.

"I thought you said we were going to be late," Delaney parried.

Keira glanced at the clock on the oven. "We are," she conceded. "Get your coat. We're almost finished." Delaney zipped off again and Keira exhaled with her forehead creased. "Precociousness has its drawbacks."

That was when he realized a roadblock in this relationship might be a pig-tail-wearing, four-foot-two inch, fifty-pound female cute enough to have him thinking about what it would be like to have children.

Fifteen minutes later they stood on the front stoop, Keira turning the key in the lock, when Dylan noticed disturbed snow under the front window. Trying not to draw attention to himself he followed the path with his eyes around the side of the house. When he glanced back he could see the subtle signs someone had been outside the house all along to the back and probably brushed something, perhaps a branch, over their footprints in an effort to hide them.

He strolled down the sidewalk with the two girls, giving Keira's hand a squeeze when he thought Delaney wasn't looking. She flashed him a smile, and he guessed she was unaware of what he saw. He opened the doors of the mid-sized sedan Keira told him she had borrowed from her brother. After Laney was safely stowed away in the back, he watched the pair whiz off. As he headed to his car, he flipped open his cell phone.

"Lieutenant Leake, speaking."

"Leake, this is Dylan Fischer, the paramedic at Keira Kelly's house?"

Dylan could almost hear him come to attention. "Yes?"

"I believe someone has been outside Mrs. Kelly's house. I saw evidence in the snow—"

"I'll be by to check it out. I can stick around there for most of the day today, between calls that is, but I can't tonight."

"Okay. Thanks for checking into it."

"Thank you, Mr. Fischer."

Dylan started the engine, but his eyes were drawn back up to the house. Someone had been outside the window he slept in front of.

He had to find a way to come back tonight.

CHAPTER ELEVEN

This is Officer Leake from the DPD, Mrs. Kelly, and I'm calling, unfortunately, to let you know your home was broken into. We need you to come home and tell us what's missing, if possible.

The words just kept sounding in Keira's mind like amplifiers after a concert. Someone had broken into her home, the home she shared with her baby girl. What did they take? True, most everything she could do without. They probably hadn't touched anything that would have been invaluable to her—like family pictures, Delaney's finger-paintings and other crafts—but she felt sick knowing someone had been in her home, the oasis she'd created to shelter them from harm after Kevin's death.

She pulled in front of her house, rolling up to the curb and peering out the window as if there would be some glaringly visible sign of the intrusion. She scanned the street and seeing no police cars, hesitated. Could this be some kind of trap? The cell-phone she had tossed into the passenger's seat rang, making her jump. As it danced and buzzed on the seat next to her purse, she glanced back up at the house warily, as if answering the phone might detonate a bomb, or cause some other calamity. She could see the number on the screen and recognized it as the one Dylan programmed into her cell earlier that morning.

"Good grief," she chastised herself, picking it up and pushing the button to receive the call. "Hi."

"Oh, Keira, good. I caught you."

She barely heard him as she caught sight of some movement behind her front windows.

"Did you speak to Officer Leake?"

"Yes. How did you know?"

"Because I called him."

"You? Did something happen after I left? You didn't get hurt or anything, did you?" Visions of him scrapping with some burly hooded figure snuck into her thoughts.

"No, of course not." He sounded irritated by the notion. "I spotted some marks in the snow outside your house, so I gave him a call. When he came out to the house he saw the back door was jimmied. While they waited for a backup team to arrive, apparently the guy heard them, or became aware of their presence somehow, because he went out an upper window, slid across the roof, and shimmied down a tree. He got away, Keira, I'm sorry. Keira? Keira, are you there?"

She stared at an upper window, where she could now see a patch of snow cleared off the roof from the window to the humongous fir tree in her front yard. Her chest tightened.

"They're sure he got away?"

"Yes," Dylan told Keira firmly, wanting to reassure her. "They followed his footprints to an alley behind your home and figured he had a car waiting there for him." He paused. "Where are you, anyway?"

"In front of the house. I didn't want to go inside in case the phone call from the police hadn't actually been from the police. It could have been a ruse to lead me back here."

"Good thinking." He sounded surprised.

She got a glimpse of the figure of a man peering out of the window upstairs. A buzz sounded in her ear. "I've got another call. Can you hold for a minute?"

"Sure."

She hurried to pick up the call. "Hello?"

"This is Officer Gary Leake. Is that you in front of the house, Mrs. Kelly?"

Keira glanced up again and saw the man in the window pull back the drapes and watch her, a phone to his ear. He didn't have a uniform on, she hesitated. Seeming to understand her trepidation, he told her. "I'll come out to the car with my badge out so you can see I really am a member of the DPD."

"Okay."

"Be down in a second."

She clicked back to Dylan, who immediately started talking. "Keira, is that you? Are you okay?"

"Fine," she exhaled, feeling a little stupid for having panicked. "Listen, Dylan, I appreciate all you've done for me, but now, with this guy breaking into my house in broad daylight... I just don't want you to get hurt."

"I won't," he huffed. He barreled on, heedless of her warning. "I've been thinking about it and it might be a good idea to have an alarm system installed—"

Keira's eyes flickered to the sidewalk where she could see the robust form of Officer Leake hustling, puffing out great clouds of his breath. He fished out his badge but she didn't even need it now. She recognized the officer from the hospital and the accident scene.

"Dylan, Officer Leake is here. I've got to go." She released her seatbelt, not even taking a peek at the badge now pressed against her passenger window.

"Okay. Call me back."

She agreed hastily and got out of the car. "Officer Leake, thank you for coming out."

"Yes, ma'am. Would you like to follow me inside now?" He accompanied her up the first set of stairs, talking as they traversed the short sidewalk. "The perpetrator came in through the back door. If you don't mind me saying, ma'am, you could use a deadbolt on there."

For the first time Keira thought about the term deadbolt and it sent a shiver up her spine. If that bolt don't work, you're dead.

"He did a little damage to the frame of the door, but nothing which couldn't be fixed with relative ease."

She climbed the steps with the police officer and a taller, thinner man opened the door so she could pass through. He smiled at her and nodded, dressed, like Leake, in a suit. She thought about how strange it felt to have someone else letting her into her own home. When she entered the living room, Keira froze in her tracks. Her eyes searched the room apprehensively, but everything remained just as it was that morning when she'd left for work.

"Anything missing?" Officer Leake prompted, seeming more sympathetic than in their last few meetings. She shook her head.

When she didn't move forward, the other policeman took the lead. "Perhaps in one of the bedrooms?"

She followed him. Both of the bedroom doors lay open, but when she went inside hers, she saw the jewelry box on the dresser, along with some cash she forgot to transfer to a wallet.

"Anything here?"

Keira walked over to the dresser and lifted the lid to her jewelry box. She owned nothing valuable outside of her wedding set, an anniversary band, and a pair of sapphire and diamond earrings Kevin purchased for her Valentine's gift several years ago. All three were readily visible.

"It's all here."

Officer Leake's face appeared serious.

"Maybe you guys got here before he had a chance to—"

"Yeah. Maybe," Leake responded, sounding unconvinced.

"What other explanation could there be?"

"What he searched for wasn't here."

"Which would be?"

Leake stared at her.

"What?"

He cleared his throat. "Have you ever felt like someone was following you? Or watching you?"

Her heart beat faster. "No."

"Ever received any mysterious phone calls where no one talks?"

"No." An unreasonable anger surfaced. "I think you're on the wrong track here."

"Mrs. Kelly, I think someone might have killed your husband to get him out of the way in order to come after you."

A wave of heat swamped Keira. A hand went down on the dresser to steady her. "What? That can't be. Kevin's death was an accident. He lost control of his car and it went over the edge of a cliff."

"Or maybe he was run off, just as someone tried to batter you in your car."

Kevin's death may not have been an accident? Her world spun off its axis.

"That's enough."

A man in a blue uniform slid into the room behind Leake. He came over to support her, his hand gripping her elbow with a gentle, yet reassuring touch.

"Are you all right?"

She blinked. It was Dylan who came to her rescue. The heat she felt seconds before turned to cold, leaving her numb.

"You look pretty pale. I think you should sit down."

"Not in here," she mumbled, the bed too high to manage. "On the couch."

He began to escort her into the next room. "Can you please get her a glass of water?" he directed Leake. "The kitchen is to the right."

Dylan got her seated on the couch and crouched down in front of her. She sat on the edge primly, her back razor-straight, muscles tensed.

"Any headache?"

"Just a little one. More like a fuzzy humming."

Leake arrived with the water and Dylan took it from the officer to hand to Keira. Her hands shook a little as she raised the glass to her lips, but the water soothed her throat, which, she now realized, felt tight.

"Better?"

She nodded.

"You look better. Your color's coming back." Dylan squeezed her knee and then rose to take the seat next to her.

"Can I ask why you're here, sir?" the other officer started, but Leake waved him off. "Ted, could you finish the fingerprinting upstairs?"

"Sure." The thinner man disappeared.

"Mrs. Kelly," Leake said kindly, "I'm sorry if my questions upset you. I'm just trying to figure this out." He hesitated a few seconds before continuing, his voice soft. "I could be wrong about what's going on here, but a man stalked my sister, a stranger she didn't even know, and he ended up killing her." She could see the pain in his eyes, the guilt she imagined he felt for not being able to save his sister. "Maybe it's just because, physically, you remind me a lot of my sister, Mrs. Kelly, but I think it's something more. Maybe I'm just obsessing too much about it. But, to be honest with you, this case has made me jumpy since the get-go. I've got a feeling this is personal somehow..." He trailed off, his mind full of possibilities. "There is no one you find a bit creepy? A janitor, maybe? Grocery clerk? Or someone who just looks at you strangely...?"

She shook her head through his whole litany. "Sorry," she said automatically, though she knew there wasn't anything to be sorry for. "This all is just so...I mean..." She set her glass down on the trunk in front of her. "If someone ran Kevin off the road, why didn't they come after me right away? Why wait eleven months? It doesn't make sense."

"Well, didn't you move right after your husband's death?"

She nodded. She hadn't been able to sleep in the house they built together. She still couldn't bear to go upstairs in this house, where the movers had put Kevin's desk and computer.

"Perhaps he couldn't find you at first. What about an ex-boyfriend?"

"Kevin and I were high school sweethearts." She unconsciously rubbed one temple with a thumb, kneading her forehead with her fingers.

"I think she needs to get some rest," Dylan interrupted.

Leake sighed, closing his notebook and tapping his pen against it in frustration. "Well, one thing we can do, Mrs. Kelly, is have a security system installed here." He reached into his pocket and pulled out a card. "This company developed the best products around. Why don't you give them a call? I'll just go check on my partner and then we'll be out of your hair in no time."

The policeman left and she stared at the card blankly.

"I think that would be a good idea. I can call if you want."

This would be just the kind of thing she would have let Kevin take care of before he died, but she was getting used to handling things herself. "No, that's okay. Thanks, Dylan." She gave his arm a squeeze and then drew her cell-phone out of her coat pocket and dialed the number.

The voice over the line sounded like a disinterested teenager. "Five Alarm Security. Tim, speaking."

"Hi. I want to talk to someone about having an alarm system installed."

"Let me check my appointment book for our next opening."

She could hear chewing noises. "The sooner you can get out here the better. Someone broke into my house today."

"We can squeeze you in a week from tomorrow."

"A week from tomorrow?" She looked up as the detectives walked back into the room. "Can't somebody come out sooner? The police seem to think the intruder might come back."

"I'm sorry. That's our first opening."

"O-okay," she answered uncertainly. Leake gestured for the phone and she handed it over with a quizzical expression.

"This is Officer Gary Leake of the Denver Police Department, who am I speaking to?" There was a pause. "Well, *Timmy*," he snickered with disgust, "Mrs. Kelly here needs an alarm system *now*!" Again a pause ensued in which Keira and Dylan watched the policeman's face turn from pink, to red, to purple. "Who's in charge there?" The policeman's eyes flicked up to hers while he listened to the answer, shaking his head in disbelief. "Put him on," he told the kid, annunciating distinctly. The next exchange had the officer turning away and screaming into the receiver. "What do you mean he's out to lunch? He's not out to lunch you pansy-assed, little liar, you're just afraid to put him on. Well I'm just gonna come down there then and—"

Leake stopped mid-sentence. He turned around slowly and handed Keira the phone. "Punk hung up on me!" he sputtered, fuming. He took a deep breath. "Listen, Mrs. Kelly, I don't want you to worry about that. I'll go down there myself and have someone out here in a jiffy. They'll also have an apology for you."

"Thank you. I appreciate all you're doing for me."

"Yes, Ma'am. Well, if you think of anything— "

"I have your card."

Dylan rose and escorted the two men to the door.

"Good news is," Leake told him in a hushed tone, though she could still hear him, "I should probably be able to get my sergeant to okay a patrol car outside for tonight."

Dylan nodded, glancing back at her. She still sat, shell shocked, on the edge of the couch.

After the policemen's departure, she flopped back onto the couch, laying her head against the cushions with a moan.

"You look spent." He climbed over her legs. "Come here," he added softly. He sat back down and shifted her so she lay against him. Without speaking he massaged her shoulders. She closed her eyes. His hands were warm and confident and just what she needed right now. She relaxed into him more as he kneaded tight muscles.

Suddenly she flew up. "You're supposed to be at work!"

He pulled her back down. "Relax. I'm on my lunch break."

"Mmm..." She felt like she could take a nap, right there in his arms. "Aren't you going to be hungry later?" she mumbled.

"I can grab something."

"I'm not going back to work," she muttered, as if the point were in question.

"Good idea."

And that was the last thought Keira had for a while.

CHAPTER TWELVE

Dylan heard the beep outside telling him his partner was back. He had nodded off, and it took him a second or two to remember where he was. He stretched, careful not to jostle Keira, and then maneuvered so he could slide out from under the weight of her body and still support her. He laid her down on the couch. His blankets still lay folded on a chair, so he spread one over her. A second beep had him hustling out the door.

A half hour later he got a call on his cell.

"Sorry I fell asleep on you, literally."

Funny how the sound of her voice already had the power to make him smile. "That's okay. I'm just sorry I had to leave. Can I make it up to you by bringing dinner over? What does Delaney like?"

"Delaney's not going to be here. I'm sending her over to spend the night at my brother's house. I didn't tell them about all this. They have enough on their plate." She paused. "I considered getting a hotel room, but then I thought, I'm not going to let this creep push me out of my own home. I don't know, maybe I'm nuts for staying here."

"I thought about that, too. The thing is, how long could you afford to stay in a hotel? And what's to say he won't find you there? Leake told me he'll have a car outside, so you don't have to worry about your safety tonight. Just give Leake a little time, Keira. He'll figure this thing out."

"I hope so." Her voice quieted and there was silence for several seconds.

His partner, Steve, had been glancing over at him, probably curious about the conversation. Dylan turned a little toward the window, creating a sort of barrier with his shoulder, and dropped his voice. "Can I still bring dinner by tonight?"

"Dylan...hanging out with me could be hazardous to your health."

He only hesitated a second. "But not being with you is driving me crazy."

He could hear her smile over the phone. "Really?"

"Really. I'll be by around...my shift ends at five...five-thirty, quarter-to-six?"

"Sounds great."

He hung up and turned forward again. He threw a sheepish look in Steve's direction, cleared his throat and pretended to look at the scenery outside the ambulance window. A minute ticked by and he thought he was off the hook.

"So who is the special lady that's putting such a big smile on your face?"

Dylan shook his head. "Just a girl I met." He shrugged then turned to gaze out the window again to avoid Steve's pointed looks. Tapping his cell-phone to his chin he thought about the two girls who so recently captured his heart.

WHEN KEIRA OPENED THE door Dylan stood on the doorstep in his uniform holding up two Chinese takeout boxes in each hand with a big bag under his arm.

"Hey, come in."

"I didn't know what you wanted, so I just got a variety."

"Sounds good. I'll get some plates down. I'm starved. I sort of forgot to eat lunch."

"Me, too."

They talked about inconsequential things while they ate, just enjoying each other's company. When they finished, he followed her to the sink to help her clean up. "It's quiet around here without Delaney."

"It sure is."

"You miss her?"

"Yeah. But I didn't want to expose her to any possible harm." Each caught up in their own thoughts, the only sound for a while was the water running into the sink. "I don't know what I'm going to do, though. I can't keep having Delaney at her cousins' all the time." She sighed.

He grabbed a towel and watched her hands sliding over the sudsy plates. "Once you get the alarm system installed, you can relax a little more. Have you heard from Leake?"

She chuckled. "He's got someone coming over here tomorrow. I'm meeting the installer after school."

"Good." He took the last plate and dried it off. "How about a movie? I've got one in my car."

"Sure." She seemed to visibly unwind a little. Her smile was more genuine, her shoulders less tense.

Dylan stepped out into the chilly night to retrieve the movie from his car. He scanned the lawn, searching for fresh prints, but it was hard to tell which ones might be new with all the footprints the police made earlier in the day. He lifted his head and caught sight of Officer Leake's car. This time it was parked on the near side of the street, almost behind a huge pine tree, in a good spot to stay hidden, but still be able to see the house well. He grabbed the movie and headed back inside.

When he got in, Keira poured a glass of wine. "Would you like a glass, too...or I still have beer somewhere...?" She opened the fridge and started searching.

"Wine is fine."

When she handed him his glass she peeked at the DVD in his hand. "Umm, 'Days to Remember'? Isn't that kind of a chick flick?"

Seeing the spark of interest in her eyes, he smiled. "Well, if you'd rather not..." He turned away from her and she made a dive for the movie.

"Are you kidding? I've been dying to see this."

A few minutes later they sat sharing a blanket on the couch. During a lull in the action she turned her face to him. "This is nice."

He kissed her softly once. "Yes. It is."

Snuggling closer to his side she settled in for the duration of the movie. When the end credits rolled, she sat up. "That's it? She's going to just leave her husband? What an idiot. He was hot."

"Oh, he was, was he?"

"Not as hot as a paramedic," she amended, playing with his top button.

"Oh, yeah, 'cause a blue button-down shirt and navy uniform pants are where it's at."

"Oh, no," she continued coyly, running a finger over the star on his chest, which caused his pulse to pick up. "Your badge is what makes the outfit."

He chuckled. "Really?"

"And it's not just that." She ran her finger down his chest. "It's the way you wear the uniform."

He played with her hair. "I think somebody's had too much to drink."

"Have you? Then you probably shouldn't drive." She sat up and finished the rest of her glass of wine.

"I'm not talking about me."

Keira looked around exaggeratedly. "Who then?"

"You, missy," he said, tweaking her nose. He stood and retrieved his own glass from an end table, taking it to the sink to rinse out. She followed behind him.

"I was trying to get you drunk so I could take advantage of you."

"That was the plan, huh?" He asked her with a raised eyebrow, his hands buried in the suds.

"Yes," she chirped with a sloppy smile.

He plucked her glass from her hands. "Well, it didn't work out quite like you thought it would, did it?"

Her smile stretched wider as she grabbed him by the hips. "Not yet."

Dylan rinsed the glass off and set it in the strainer, drying his hands on a nearby towel and turning in her arms. He kissed her. He meant to take it easy, but she drew him in deeper. He felt the hours of waiting to be with her, thinking of her as he worked his shift, remembering the soft feel of her skin when she'd sat in his lap the night before. With a groan he switched angles so he could take the kiss even deeper, sliding his hands up and down her arms.

"Dylan," she whispered. "We're all alone now. Delaney's not here."

She was running through his veins, but he closed his eyes and took a deep breath. "I should go."

"What? You're going to leave me here alone?"

"There's a squad car right outside."

"I didn't see one," she spouted, her forehead wrinkling.

He took her by the shoulders and gently spun her around, guiding her to the dark front room. "See, there?" He pointed. "Under the pine tree? You can see just the nose of a navy car."

"Oh," she sounded disappointed. "Well, I guess if you have to go." She flopped down on the couch and planted her elbows on her knees, head on her fists as if thinking. He lowered himself down beside her.

"So, that's it. You were just using me for my manly ability to protect you?"

She turned to him quickly. "No. Oh, gosh, Dylan, no. It isn't that."

Gazing into her face something dissolved inside of him. "Then what?" he asked softly.

"Well," she replied, ducking her head as if embarrassed, "when you said over the phone not being with me was driving you crazy..."

"Uh-huh."

"Well...not being with you was kind of driving me crazy, too." She looked up into his eyes. "When I fell asleep in your arms earlier today, it felt so good. And looking forward to seeing you tonight is what got me through the afternoon."

"Why, Miss Keira," Dylan said, adopting a Southern accent, and sweeping her hair off her face with one hand, "I do believe that's the sweetest thing you've ever said to me." With that he kissed her full on the mouth. He reclined on the couch, pulling her over him so she gazed down into his face. Her red hair fell forward and he marveled at its color in the streetlight, a silky swatch of fire licking her face, smooth and satiny.

He cupped his hand behind her neck and pulled her in again for a kiss. He could feel the heat spread along his body as his hands wandered over denim, up her legs and over her tush, finding skin and sliding over it to feel the curve of shoulder blades. All the while a voice screamed in his head, "I want this, I need this, now, and every day." Her body writhed against his, responding to his touch.

She pulled away, extending her arms to look him in the eye. "Stay with me tonight, Dylan. Please stay."

That was all the encouragement he needed. Sitting up, he shifted her onto his lap. Her hands lay on either side of his face as her lips sought his time and again. Cradling her in his arms, he lifted her and carried her to the bedroom, using his foot to open the crack in the door wider. The door swung loosely on its hinges causing the doorknob to crash into the wall.

"Sorry."

"That's okay," she mumbled between kisses, her arms now looped around his neck. "It happens all the time."

He deposited her on the bed. She shifted to her knees, running hands up his chest.

"Are you sure you want to do this?" He wouldn't take advantage of her if the wine might be influencing her behavior.

She smiled at him wickedly, unbuttoning his shirt with maddening slowness. "Are you sure *you* want to do this?"

He returned the smile. "Oh, yeah. Damn sure."

He pushed her back on the bed, falling on top of her with a playful growl. He adjusted so he could whip off his shirt. Her hands hungrily explored his chest and arms. He tugged at her sweater—she had abandoned the belt when they curled up on the couch earlier—and pulled it off to discover the bounty beneath. His hands filled with her, skimming over lace and satin and relishing the first feel of her curves, the tautness of her stomach. Without prelude he slid his hands under the waistband of her jeans, beneath her panties, feeling her warmth. She moaned and arched her back and he was thrilled by the power he possessed to pleasure her.

She fumbled with his pants, and frustrated by the restriction of clothes, he scooted off her, grasping the waistline of her jeans and panties and pulling them off as one. In seconds he abandoned his clothes and came to her, wanting her fiercely, but holding back. Unlike with other women, he found his need to give to her stronger than his need to take from her. He saw the pain of someone who had lost before in her eyes, and he wanted to erase it. All he wanted to see in those eyes was a need for him.

He slid up her, kissing her soft skin as he ascended, taking her up at the same time, his hands gentler now, more controlled. They soothed and excited at the same time. He pushed back the edges of her bra and took her nipple into his mouth. The scrape of teeth over sensitive flesh, the comforting yet teasing pain as he sucked, took her over the edge. She melted into the mattress, what was once all motion, completely still. He rested with her, allowing her body time to relax and when he touched, and stroked and titillated again, she cried out to him.

"Dylan, I need you, now!"

He was incapable of denying her urgent request and as they coupled, the tension lessened a little and they eased again into a deep kiss. When his hips began to move she matched his rhythm, swaying with him, melded as one. As his motions became more intense she clenched his flesh, drawing him deeper into her, urging her body closer, though they could be no closer. The pace increased little by little until they released together and Dylan lay heavily on her chest. When he pulled away, ending the connection, a little sigh escaped her, but Dylan grabbed her hand, holding it in the dark. Neither one spoke as they brought their breathing back down to normal.

Dylan turned to her. "Come here." He raised an arm and she placed her head on his chest, wriggling closer. He thought about what to say. It was too early for "I love you," and "that was nice" sounded lame. "That was incredible" sounded hokey, although those were the words on his lips as they fell asleep.

CHAPTER THIRTEEN

Keira woke to an empty bed. Stretching like a cat she felt Dylan's warmth still, could smell his scent on the sheets. She needed to see him. She jumped out of bed and grabbed her silk Japanese robe. But stepping out of the bedroom she didn't expect to find him in the position he was in. Lying on his side, he fiddled with something black hanging from the bottom of the back door, which lay partially open. She hugged her robe closer, a question on her pursed lips, when he turned his head.

"Oh, hi," he blurted out, appearing startled. He added quickly, "I was just fixing your door." He swung up to sit cross-legged on the floor, beaming at her.

"I see that. I didn't even know it was broken down there."

"Oh, it's not." Perhaps seeing the confused expression on her face, he explained, "It's just...I noticed a gap...and it let in cold air. So I brought some insulation tape. Let me just finish up and I'll come over there and give you a hug."

She smiled, pleased it felt so natural with him. "I'll start breakfast." She turned and trekked back into the kitchen, wondering what ingredients she could find there which, when thrown together, might make a meal. When he came in she already had bacon and juice on the table and eggs getting ready to come out of the skillet.

She turned to catch him grinning, holding up a package. "I brought a deadbolt, too, but I thought the whole drilling through the door thing might wake you up."

"Yeah, there's always that chance," she joked.

He came over and wrapped his arms around her waist. "You look gorgeous in the morning."

Her hands went to her hair, trying to pat it down. "Oh, I'm embarrassed."

He swung her hips from side to side. "No, I mean it." He kissed her cheek and then nuzzled her ear. "You smell good, too."

She giggled as his whiskers tickled. He swiped a piece of bacon from the table. "Mmm...this is great." She liked his free and easy nature. No awkwardness like she might have expected the morning after. Then she started to wonder just how many morning afters he had experienced. Maybe that was why this came without effort to him. With her it had only been Kevin. Always, Kevin...

Dylan was talking about something, but all of a sudden she couldn't hear him. On automatic, she reached into the fridge to get butter for the toast, but when she closed it she stood staring at the picture of the sunflower magnetized to the door. "Luf u Mommy and Daddy." Her little girl, *their* little girl, Kevin and hers...her bedroom, just a few feet away. The horror of what she had done hit her. *Delaney's out of the house for one night and I'm taking a man to my bedroom who I've only known for a few days*?

"I can't do this," she mumbled.

He looked up from the table. "What?"

"I can't do this," she said louder, gripping the counter.

"What, make breakfast? That's okay. I can just grab something—"

She whirled on him. "I can't do this, Dylan. This is not who I am."

He stared at her. "Can't do what?"

"Can't do this!" she screamed, gesturing wildly between them. "Sleep with you."

He moved his mouth for a few seconds before words came out, his eyes searching her. "You...I don't understand."

"It's not who I am. I'm not some girl you can woo into the back of your ambulance and—"

He held his hands up. "Whoa, whoa, whoa! I did not woo you...I mean, you seemed pretty fine with things last night."

"I was drunk."

He seemed stunned. "Keira, what happened...?"

"Look, I'm just not the kind of girl who climbs into the back of ambulances, or whatever, and screws the cute paramedic."

"First of all, you've got a very warped image of what goes on in the back of an ambulance—"

"I don't want to be one in a string of many. I mean I'm sure you are used to this, but—"

His face clouded. "What? Sleeping around?"

"Yes."

He pushed his chair from the table, grabbing his coat from off its back where he left it the night before. His jaw was tight as he strode toward the front door, but then he stopped in the archway between the dining room and kitchen.

"For the record, I don't do this either," he said without turning, his voice subdued. "I've only been in a couple of relationships that ended up...intimately, and those girls I dated for several months."

Keira stood there as he walked away, feeling as though she had been clothes-lined. The sound of the front door opening set her in motion.

"Wait. Wait!" She ran to catch him. He stood frozen in the doorway, his hand still on the doorknob. "Wait," she pleaded, her voice now weak. "I'm sorry."

He turned, finally, and she began to shake, tears rolling down her face. "I'm so sorry. It's just...I'm not used to this. This is all new to me. There was only Kevin." Speaking his name was like opening a floodgate. She began to sob.

DYLAN STOOD TRANSFIXED for a second, his ire dropping from him piece-by-piece. Soon the anger gave way to guilt. He should have taken things slower, knowing her vulnerability, and not only because of having recently lost her husband. She had also been attacked by someone and her home broken into. One look into those eyes as she stood, weeping, before him, and he threw his coat on a chair and crossed the room to take her in his arms. "Shh...don't do that."

"I'm sorry," she mumbled over and over again into his chest. "I shouldn't have said those things."

"Hey. Hey, now. Come on, stop that." He sighed. "This is all new to me, too, Keira, because...I've never felt for any woman the things I feel for you."

She lifted her head, a hint of a smile peeking through the tears. "Really?"

He laughed. "Really." He kissed her forehead and then pulled her close. They stood that way for several seconds without speaking.

Her voice came from his chest. "I'm sorry about my little meltdown." She pulled her head back to peer up at him. "I guess I can get pretty emotional."

He chuckled, kissing her tearstained cheeks. "That's okay. I love all of you. Even your emotional parts."

She laid her head back down, seeming unwilling to part from him.

"Now, as much as I hate to, I should probably get going."

"What about breakfast?"

"Well..." He hesitated, doing some quick mental calculations. "Okay, but it has to be fast because I need to get back to my place and take a shower before work."

They walked hand and hand back to the breakfast table but the awkwardness was there now and remained until he kissed her goodbye at the door and left.

CHAPTER FOURTEEN

A half-hour into their shift, Dylan and Steve got their first call of the day. Eighty-three-year-old male with chest pains. Rolling up to the apartment complex, Dylan admired the building over his shoulder as he reached into a side storage bin to pull out his bag. Though appearing older, it was well kept and the owners had given it a Southwestern flair by painting buildings either mustard yellow, avocado green, or rust orange. The overall effect was cheerful. A woman who appeared to be in her early sixties was waving at them from a doorway. She wore a Mumu-style dress and her bottle-red, curly hair bobbed up and down in the wind despite the ribbon tied at the nape of her neck which tried to keep it in place.

"Thank you for coming," she said when they reached her. "My name's Kathy Ryan. I'm the landlady here. I'll lead you up there. It's the Reinbecks." She held the door so they could get the gurney through, then, started climbing the inner stairs ahead of them.

"Both of them?" Steve queried.

"No. Just Ed. Though Hettie's blood pressure must be through the roof."

They reached a second floor apartment, whose door lay open.

"Well, hallo there," a cheerful voice called out when they entered. From a worn, navy blue recliner a man with patchy grey hair smiled at them. An oxygen tank was set up to his right and a nasal cannula tube ran from it to his shoulder before looping around his head. "How ya fellows doin'?" he asked in a raspy voice, one hand resting lightly on a four-pronged quad-cane in front of him.

"Good...Mr. Reinbeck, is it?" Dylan responded. He generally took the lead in assessing the patients, as he was senior, and Steve preferred the driving end. It had taken him a while to learn to trust the stunt driver-like maneuvers of his partner, but after four months, they worked together like a pair of veterans, anticipating each other's moves and playing off their individual strengths and weaknesses in the field. He bent down in front of the older man, taking in his color, sunken cheeks, and the surprising twinkle in his eyes. "I think the question is... how are *you* doing?" He noted a bead of sweat on the man's forehead and along his top lip as he wheezed in.

"Oh, fine. Fine." He smiled as he said it, as if they had just arrived for a cup of coffee. He leaned forward, bringing a hand to his mouth conspiratorially, "The old lady's overreacting."

His eyes roamed to the man's puffy hand on his cane and the bruises there. Already on blood thinners, then. His fingertips were clubbed, which proved him a chronic smoker. The fingers had grown in an effort to take in more oxygen. The apartment didn't have that stale smoke smell, though. His eyes darted to the balcony, no tell-tale coffee can to hold cigarette butts, so he probably didn't smoke out there, either. Glancing around he spotted two amber colored, heavy ashtrays on end tables, but they were polished clean. Former smoker then. "Mind if I take your pulse?"

"Oh, sure, sure." Ed held out his wrist accommodatingly. He glanced up at Steve. "Ya want some toast or somethin'?"

He smiled. "No, sir. I'm fine."

A voice called from the hall behind them. "Here they are, Ed." A lady rushed into the room holding a pair of men's dress shoes. She wore a simply cut, quarter-sleeved solid black dress, a strand of pearls at her throat. Upon catching sight of the two paramedics she said, "Well now, it's about time you got here."

Dylan caught Steve's change of posture out of the corner of his eye and knew his partner had bristled at the accusation. *It took us less than seven minutes to arrive after the phone call was received by the dispatcher. That can seem like an eternity, though, when you are worried about someone.* He'd worked the job long enough to know sometimes concerned people lashed out just to keep their other emotions under control.

"Now, Momma," Ed hushed, "is that any way to treat our guests?"

"Yeah," Kathy added with a grin, coming over to pat the older man's arm. "Ed here just offered them toast."

Mrs. Reinbeck's stern face went through a slow metamorphosis and she giggled. "He didn't."

"He did," Kathy verified.

"What? Everybody likes toast. Don't you, boys?"

"Yes, sir," they both answered.

Dylan half-listened to the conversation but was really more focused on the sound of his patient's breathing. And there it was. The rattle which told him the elderly man had fluid in his lungs. This, combined with Mr. Reinbeck's thready pulse had him concerned.

He reached for the oximeter Steve had ready and carefully clipped it on the man's finger. "Mr. Reinbeck, why did you call us today?"

"*I* didn't call you. My blushing bride did." He jerked his thumb in his wife's direction, straining the cord to the pulse/ox reader.

Mrs. Reinbeck ignored the remark, talking over him. "He just didn't look right. He was dizzy and short of breath—"

Her husband took the opportunity to grab her hand and look up at her fondly. "That's because you always take my breath away, Hettie dear."

She rolled her eyes. "Yes, sure, whatever. He didn't eat well this morning—"

Mr. Reinbeck looked up at the other men for support. "I wasn't hungry. Can't a man not be hungry every once in a while?"

"—and he always eats well, as you can see." She patted his paunch, though the rest of him was skin and bones. "And he just didn't look right. Don't you think his color is off?"

"Your absolutely correct, Mrs. Reinbeck—" Dylan responded.

"Traitor," Ed Reinbeck muttered.

"—his oxygen saturation level is eighty-two percent, even with the oxygen he's receiving. I'd like to take him into the ER—"

"Oh, come on," Ed protested.

"—to get looked over. And on the way there, we'll take an EKG to see how his heart's doing."

Steve stepped forward. "Mr. Reinbeck, we're going to help you onto the gurney now. Do you think you can stand?"

"Of course, I can stand. What kind of question is that? 'Can you stand?' I'm not an invalid," he grumbled.

Dylan and Steve bookended him, Dylan pulling along the oxygen tank, but the older man was surprisingly agile. He stormed—as far as an eighty-three-year-old with a cane can storm—over to the gurney, gave a little hop, and had his backside on the bed. The two paramedics tried to help him, but he pretty much swung his legs up and reclined by himself, crossing arms over chest defiantly, and staring at the ceiling. Dylan nestled the oxygen tank in beside their patient, and Steve secured the sides of the bed.

Dylan turned to Mrs. Reinbeck. "I'd like you to ride along with us in the ambulance if you could and help fill out a health history questionnaire for your husband and answer any questions that he might not be able to."

"I'm right here," Ed mumbled.

"Yes, sir. Sometimes there are things that one spouse will remember that the other one forgets—" Dylan tried to explain.

"I want my *TV Guide*. If I've got to be in the damn hospital, I want to know what channels to turn to."

Dylan turned to check the TV stand by the chair, but all he saw was a glass of water. He saw the corner of something sticking out of the cushions.

"Edward Andrew Reinbeck," Hettie interjected. "You are acting like a baby."

"I am not, woman."

When Dylan yanked out the TV Guide, a cigar rolled out with it. It was evident that the end had been lit at one point and he now noted several small burn marks in the chair's cushion. He stuck the cigar in his pocket subtly and turned from the chair.

"Mrs. Reinbeck, if you'd like to get your purse, we'll wait and walk with you downstairs."

"Just call me Hettie." She bent and gave her husband a peck on the cheek, then hurried off.

When she stepped into a bedroom he turned to Ed. "Mr. Reinbeck, have you been smoking cigars?"

"What?" he blustered.

He slipped the cigar from his pocket as proof.

"Oh, Ed," Kathy chastised.

"Just every once in a while. Look, I'm not stupid. I know I don't have a lot of days left. But I'm not dead yet, and I like to enjoy a cigar every once in a while."

"Eddie!" Unbeknownst to anyone, Hettie Reinbeck had returned to the hallway and spotted the cigar. Belatedly, Dylan hid it behind his back. "How could you?"

"Now, Hettie..."

She scowled at him. "When? When did you do this? I'm here with you all of the time."

"That's not important—"

"It's when the Ringwold boy comes over, isn't it? When I go grocery shopping."

"Now, Mother—"

"Don't you 'now, Mother,' me. Answer me!"

Ed stubbornly refused to tell his wife. Dylan stood shifting his weight from one foot to the other, feeling bad for having started the tiff. "Uhh, ma'am, we should probably get your husband to the hospital now."

The woman frowned at him for a second, hands on hips, then turned her attention back to her husband. "On oxygen even. You could have blown this whole place to Kingdom Come!"

"I turned the oxygen off."

"Well. How diligent of you."

"Umm...Hettie," the landlady interrupted, "I think the paramedic here is right about getting Eddie down to the ER."

Hettie's eyes flashed up to her and Dylan watched Kathy cringe slightly and take a step back. After a beat, however, Hettie gave her head a sharp nod and turned toward the door, calling over her shoulder, "Bring the old reprobate or leave him. I don't care which."

Eddie smiled confidently and brought his hands up to fold behind his head, easing back into his pillow with the pulse/ox wire running along his arm. As they started toward the door, Dylan whispered, "Sorry about that, Mr. Reinbeck."

"Not to worry, son. She's crazy about me!" he yelled the last part as loud as he could with his diminished lung capacity, sending him into a coughing fit.

"I wouldn't count on it," they heard from the hall.

Eddie winked at Dylan, Steve, and Kathy. When he got his coughing under control he reassured them. "I'll have the pants charmed off her before we hit 57th Street." He chuckled and began to cough again.

True to his word, Ed Reinbeck had his wife giggling before they even left the parking lot. Hettie sat beside Dylan while he asked her questions about Ed's health history. Then he started an IV and hooked up leads to Ed's chest from a portable EKG machine, sending the results to the hospital electronically, noting that the heart rate was elevated, in tachycardia.

As he rolled Ed into the ER, someone hollered, "Why, Edward Reinbeck. I thought I told you never to darken these doors again." A large African American woman in purple scrubs ambled over to them, giving Ed's arm a squeeze.

The older man grabbed her hand and brought it to his lips. "Dorothea Jones. Don't you look lovely today?"

"Uh-huh. Don't you try that ol' sweet talkin' on me. What he in for, Hettie?"

"The usual. Oh, and caught him smoking a cigar."

"You didn't. Um-um-um. You been a naughty boy, Ed." She smiled at Dylan. "Room Three."

"Aww, now." Ed called to Hettie as he was wheeled away. "I thought you'd forgiven me for that." But Hettie was already talking to another nurse, who also seemed to recognize the couple, and was handing her a clipboard with paperwork on it.

Dylan rolled the stretcher alongside the bed, lowering both beds' sides to get ready to transfer his patient. "EKG come through fine?"

"Yes." Dorothea took the IV bag, which was lying on the gurney, and attached it to a stand.

"It's just Hettie overreacting again."

Dorothea bent down and whispered in his ear loud enough for Dylan to hear, "Now you know Miss Hettie there is the brains of this operation, Ed." He chuckled. She rose and looked at him, eyebrows raised and chin set. "You listen to your wife, you hear?"

"Yeah, sure. Like she gives me a choice."

Dylan and the nurse got Ed into the bed with relative ease. He began to remove his equipment, noticing his patient was wearing a huge grin, eyes soft. He followed the man's gaze and saw Ed was ogling his wife.

"Quite a looker, ain't she?"

He paused, his foot on the bed's release brake. In his mind he did the reverse of what they do when they age a photo of a runaway child to give an idea of what they currently look like. The years rolled away from Hettie Reinbeck. She had a full figure and lively blue eyes and he was sure she was extremely attractive in her day.

"How long have you two been married?"

"Sixty-three years next Thursday."

"No kidding? Congratulations."

The older man turned his eyes on Dylan. "You got yourself a girl—" He squinted at Dylan's name tag, "—Dylan Fischer?"

"No, sir. Not exactly."

"How old are you?"

"Twenty-eight."

"Twenty-eight!" He tsked, but then seemed to reconsider his admonition. "Well, I guess they do things different these days, don't they, Dorothea?'

"Umm-hmm." The nurse placed a blood pressure cuff around his arm.

"You take it from me son, find yourself a girl. I know you think you've got all the time in the world, but I assure you in a snap of your fingers you're going to be blowing out eighty candles on your birthday cake—"

"Umm-hum," Dorothea added.

"Get yourself a girl."

Dylan grinned. "Yes, sir."

He took his leave, but three hours later he was bringing in another patient and decided, on a whim, to stop by and check on Ed. He noted that the third exam room was empty and walked up to the nurses' station.

"Hey, could you tell me what room Edward Reinbe—" His eyes landed on a glass door across from the station and his mouth hung open. Inside he caught a glimpse of Hettie Reinbeck with her arms around Dorothea Jones, who was sobbing uncontrollably into the older woman's bosom. Kathy hung back, dabbing at the corner of her eyes with a crumpled tissue. Hettie's eyes were wet, but she was patting Dorothea on the back and speaking to her.

"He didn't make it," the nurse manning the station explained unnecessarily.

CHAPTER FIFTEEN

Keira found it hard to concentrate at work.

"Mrs. Kelly, can you please tie my shoe?"

"Sure, Branch." She sighed, bending down to the child's level. "Okay. Come a little closer now and we'll do it together. Make two rabbit ears...good. Now the bunny runs around the tree...and pops in the hole. Now pull it tight. ...You did it!"

"I did it!" the child exclaimed, his face shining with joy.

"You sure did. I'll get a star for you to put on your chart." She made her way back to the desk, patting heads and halting abruptly as children ran across her path without looking at where they were going. The teacher in her went on auto-pilot, calling out instructions purely out of habit. "Stevie, don't climb on that... Claranne, on the paper *only*. Do *not* draw on Allison." But her thoughts were miles away with a man in a blue uniform. The gold star she peeled off the paper to give to Branch even reminded her of Dylan and she wondered, for about the bazillionth time, why she was so caught up in this man already.

It's because I'm feeling bad about the things I said this morning. No, it's because I'm feeling bad for getting carried away last night. But it was hard to feel sorry for something which felt so wonderful. Physically, sure, but also in her heart. Then she would think of Delaney and feel as if she had betrayed her daughter. *What kind of woman just falls in bed with a man she hardly knows*?

But another voice, which became more persistent, would say, *But I know everything I need to know about Dylan. He's kind*—she thought of his gentle care at the accident site. *He's good with Delaney, and surely she could only benefit from having a man like him in her life.* She flashed back to him talking with Delaney over dolls. *He's thoughtful.* A vision of him on the floor, fixing her door. *He's good with his hands.* That was when her thoughts drifted to dark, sensual places the two of them visited together, until a little pair of hands tugged on her pants.

"Mrs. Kelly, I have to go to the bathroom."

"Oh! Okay, Juan, but Jimmy's in there."

"But I have to go *now*."

She raised her head and catching the eye of her aide, indicated she would be leaving the room for a minute. She took Juan to the bigger restroom outside their classroom. As she waited for her charge, she let out a long breath, leaning against the wall with her arms crossed. At the other end of the hall she spied a door with a slim, rectangular window to one side. When she peaked out, wondering if the snow had started again, she saw a red emergency vehicle parked directly outside. Her first thought was, who needed an ambulance? Her next was to wonder if maybe Dylan came to see her.

She chastised herself. *Of course he's not waiting out there. I all but called him a man-whore this morning and then fell apart all over him.*

"Finished."

She looked down at the smiling, round, brown face of the little boy standing beside her.

"Did you wash your hands?"

With a large sigh, and a rolling of the eyes, a precursor to his teenaged days, Juan whirled around and thudded back into the bathroom. She heard the water running and suppressed a laugh. Again something drew her eyes outside, but she saw nothing new to answer her questions. Soon she was whisking Juan away to Story Hour, and her voice drifted into the hall, rising and falling with the different characters in a story about dragons and princesses.

When the final bell rang and the children rushed out the doors, she turned to clean up her room.

"Keira, don't worry about this, I've got it. You're still recovering from your accident. Just go home."

She crossed the room to give her aide a squeeze. "You're the best, Jenna. I owe you." She grabbed her bag and headed to the parking lot.

As she neared the end of the hall, she could see Dylan leaning against the grill of his rig, arms crossed in front of him, feet stretched out on the pavement. She swallowed, admiring the view. He possessed a certain self-confidence which was extremely attractive, not to mention a body most women would fantasize over. Another paramedic sat next to him on the chrome bumper. With jet black hair, his head was turned and he was laughing at something Dylan said. The peculiarly warm day had caused a lot of the snow from the previous weeks to begin melting away, so Keira guessed they were trying to take advantage of the relatively nice weather.

The door made a loud creaking sound as she left the building which apparently carried across the parking lot as Dylan turned and seeing her, straightened up. She barely caught the other paramedic mouthing, "Is that her?" She had eyes only for Dylan.

"Hi."

"Hi, there."

"What are you doing here?"

The other paramedic, who Keira did not look at, nor did Dylan acknowledge, slunk off with a muttered, "Wel-l-l-l then, I guess I'll leave you two alone."

"I came to ask you out on a date."

Her smile broadened. "A date?"

He nodded, his smile just as wide. "A real, genuine, bona fide date. Good night kiss included, if you play nice."

"Mmm...how can I resist?"

"Mommy!"

Keira turned her head and noticed, for the first time, a familiar car across the parking lot. Jeanie, her sister-in-law, was just climbing out.

But Delaney, who must have unbuckled in record time, bolted across the blacktop toward her. "Lane!" She had to place a hand behind her in the snow to keep from being pushed over as Delaney barreled into her. "How are you?"

"Good." She glanced up. "Dylan!"

He bent and picked her up, while at the same time helping Keira to her feet. "Hey, Squirt. How've ya been?"

Keira glanced back in the direction Laney appeared from and saw Jeanie strolling toward them with her hands in her pockets, grinning. She approached her sister-in-law. "Hey! Thanks so much for bringing her here."

"No problem. Who's tall, dark, and hunky?"

"Oh, that's Dylan. He's the paramedic who helped me after the accident."

But Jeanie nodded her head. "I thought it might be the infamous Dylan. Laney hasn't stopped talking about him. Is it true you two had a sleepover?" she queried, nudging Keira suggestively.

"Shut up. No. I mean, he did spend the night, but the weather was bad—"

"Sunday night? Come on. The weather wasn't so bad that a big, strapping, handsome guy like Dylan couldn't find his way home." Jeanie eyed him appreciatively as he approached with Delaney on his hip. "If I wasn't married to your brother..." she whispered under her breath. Keira smacked her arm.

"Hello," Jeanie called. She held out her hand. "I'm Jeanie McDonald, Keira's sister-in-law. You must be Dylan, the one who played dolls with Delaney."

"I am one and the same," he responded, coloring a little.

"You, uh, stopped by to check on Keira?" Jeanie asked, none too subtly. Keira shot her a look.

"Yes. And, to ask her out on a date." He gave Jeanie a charming smile.

"Oh. Really?" Jeanie seemed taken aback by his straightforwardness.

"You asked Mommy out?" Delaney questioned. Her eyes widen at first, but then she covered a laugh with her mittened hand.

"And what did she say?" Jeanie prompted.

His eyes danced. He was obviously enjoying himself. "She didn't exactly give me an answer."

All eyes turned to her expectantly. "I told him I wasn't sure," she teased.

Dylan winked at Jeanie. "She's playing hard to get. I'll just have to ask my other favorite girl out then. How's about it, Lane? Will you go out to dinner with me tonight?"

"Sure."

"Hmm. I guess I'll have to chaperone then, as Laney is far too young to go out on a date unescorted."

He sighed exaggeratedly. "Well, if you must." He addressed Jeannie, "Nice meeting you." He turned and ambled back toward his vehicle chatting away with his "date."

"He's hot!" Jeanie fanned herself.

"I know." Keira glided in his direction, leaving Jeanie in her wake.

After she'd gotten a couple of yards away she turned around. "Oh, Jeanie." Her sister-in-law glanced back. "I'll drop Delaney back by around eight."

"Sure thing."

"Thanks, sis."

She winked. "You got it."

CHAPTER SIXTEEN

Max Gerardi drove past the house again. He noted the paramedic's beat-up car outside and grimaced. That clown was making it hard for him to make any headway. Not to mention he'd seen an alarm company's van outside that very afternoon. An alarm on the house now, too. What was he going to do?

Never mind. He needed to get in and erase the evidence from Kevin Kelly's computer. That was all there was to it.

The broker still remembered the day Kevin discovered he had been ripping off some of the clients. Max had made the stupid, stupid mistake of leaving some papers in the copier, and by the time he got back to it, Kevin held the incriminating evidence in his stinking, law-abiding hands. Any other broker and it would have been okay, but brilliant Kevin suspected something right away, with only a quick glance at the numbers.

Maybe it was the fact that Kevin's office was situated adjacent to his that had done him in. Surely Kevin could have heard that loud-mouthed Vince Treetoni the afternoon he and Max had gone over his stocks together.

"I see you steered me wrong on Albacorp," the old man hollered, too deaf to believe anyone else could hear.

"Yes, Mr. Treetoni. I'm sorry about that."

"Oh, that's okay, boy. Tell me how the others have done."

The old coot always trusted him implicitly. Never questioned when Max asked him to put power of attorney into his hands so he could "get in on those hot stocks without having to waste time" getting the old goat's approval. So, with a little fancy pencil work, he'd made prosperous companies seem like they were going under and pocketed the profits himself. His "creative accounting" would be easy to find if anyone looked really hard, but no one had ever questioned it.

Until the day Kevin Kelly found his doctored papers.

When it came down to it, what happened to Kevin was really a matter of self-defense; it was him or Kevin, as simple as that.

After he'd killed Kevin, he had offered to clean out his office for the firm, searching everywhere for the papers he so desperately needed to get back. But they weren't there. Anywhere. That's when searched the computer and discovered Kevin had scanned the papers in and e-mailed a copy to himself at home. So his nightmare wasn't over. If his widow ever discovered those papers and turned them back over to someone at the brokerage, Max could wind up in prison. While some days that almost seemed appealing, anywhere to get away from that harpy of a wife of his, he entertained no real desire to go there.

In a way, killing Kevin Kelly had been the most liberating thing he had ever done in his miserable life. That, and stealing boatloads of money from people who inherited it but were too stupid to recognize an asset, even if one waddled on over and sat down in their laps. If he was discovered, after killing Kevin, Max knew just how easy it was to get rid of his problems. Just a flick of the wrist and he could steer someone into oblivion. It was fantastic. Lately he'd been thinking of even offing his wife.

Wife or not, his current problem was strolling around inside the house right now with the light on. They were probably hunched over the computer even at this moment. Every day that passed could be the day that he was discovered. There simply was no question about it; he had to get into the house tonight.

CHAPTER SEVENTEEN

They ate an early dinner, since Dylan needed to do his Santa thing at seven, and then went to stroll around the Denver Zoo looking at Zoolights, the organization's Christmas display. Fat snowflakes began to fall as they followed the lighted pathways, turning the night into a living Christmas card. The crisp, fresh air pinkened their cheeks without biting. Dylan enjoyed their time together immensely. As he strolled along, holding Keira's hand, Delaney ran ahead full of enthusiasm.

"This is great." Keira's voice was laced with contentment.

"Yes, it is," he agreed, giving her hand a squeeze. He glanced over at her, loving the cute off-white, knit beret which sat on her head at a rakish angle, and the way the snowflakes held on to her eyelashes like children who cling to their parents at bedtime. Peeking ahead, he noted Delaney seemed enthralled with the penguin display, so he stole a kiss. Keira's lips were warm and inviting, despite the temperature, and a tingle of desire zinged through him as they parted, her grey eyes laughing at him.

As they left, he looked up to see the clouds had scurried off, and the night sky had turned crystal clear, the stars competing with the hundreds of white lights the employees of the Denver Zoo hung in the trees. They bought hot chocolate from a vendor and sipped it as they headed to their cars. Keira secured Delaney into the booster seat and closed the door, leaning against her car.

"I had a great time."

He played with a strand of her hair. "I did, too."

She looked down, swiping her foot across the newly-fallen snow. "What about the kiss you promised me?" She raised her head, squinting a little in the parking lot's bright lights. "I've been good."

He glanced in the car window. "What about Delaney?"

"Well...if you plan on sticking around and kissing me some more, she should probably get used to it."

He stepped forward, pressing his lower body against hers, placing one hand on the car window. He moved in a fraction at a time, his eyes moving from her eyes to her lips and back. "Well, I do plan on kissing you some more."

"Good."

She tilted her head and he brought his lips to hers, the kiss soft and intense. When he pulled away it seemed to take her awhile to come up from where he sent her, deep within herself. Her eyes opened slowly and she smiled.

"Will I see you later?"

"Can I come by after I get off?"

"I was hoping you would."

He gave her one last kiss. "Drive safely."

"I will." She got behind the wheel and he watched her leave before getting into his car.

He thought about her all during his shift at the mall, even accidentally calling one child by her name. He hurried so much to get back to her house he forgot to change out of his clothes again.

"Why, Santa," she teased when she opened the door to him, "aren't you a bit early? You still have a week yet."

"But, I've heard you've been exceptionally good," he growled as he pushed his way in. He covered her mouth with his as he wrapped her up with one arm and used the other to shut the door behind him. He pressed her against the closet door, taking what he'd waited all night for, just a taste of her.

"Oh, Santa," she moaned.

"Ho-ho-ho," he bellowed into the fold of her neck, sending her into a girlish peal of laughter.

He walked with her into the living room, their lips still searching for and finding one another desperately as they skirted the coffee table trunk. Reaching the couch, he pulled her down onto his lap. "What do you want for Christmas, little girl?" he asked in his best dirty old man imitation.

"A ring," she responded, her voice bright.

"Hmm," he replied, surprised. She seemed to realize belatedly what her request sounded like.

"I mean, a car. Mine's pretty banged up and I need a new one."

He shook his head. "You said a ring."

"I meant jewelry."

"You said 'a ring,'" he repeated pointedly.

"Dylan, I'm sorry. I blurted out the first thing that came to my head."

"And the first thing that came to your head was a ring." She squirmed on his lap. "Never mind," he said, bending her back against the couch pillows and kissing her again.

"Mmm...I missed you."

"And I missed you." He let his hands wander to her breasts under the scoop-necked, green sweater she wore.

She began to unbutton his Santa suit but he grabbed her hands. "Wait. Wait!"

"What?" Keira asked, her eyes wide.

"I promised myself I would sleep on the couch tonight. After our...misunderstanding this morning, I don't want to push you too hard into anything you're not ready for."

She smiled, relaxing and leaning into him to kiss his neck. "I'm ready. I'm ready."

"No. Keira, no. I mean it. No funny business tonight." He unceremoniously pushed her legs off his lap. "No matter how much you tempt me."

Seeing the look in her eyes which told him she intended to rise to that challenge, he stood up quickly. "I was thinking...what's upstairs?"

"What?" She seemed completely thrown this time.

"What's upstairs? The cops said they found the intruder upstairs when they arrived. What was he doing up there?"

She shrugged. "All that's up there is Kevin's desk and computer, and maybe some files. I haven't even been up there yet. But I'm sure there's nothing of value."

"Hmm. Mind if I take a look around up there?"

"No," she answered, but the word came out strangely. Still, she got up and led him to the door which opened onto an uncarpeted staircase. She switched on a light at the bottom of the steps and only hesitated a second before climbing the short set of stairs.

That was when Dylan understood. This would have seemed to Keira like Kevin's room, and that would undoubtedly be hard. As their heads came level with the floor, he took in a large black desk with shelves and file drawers. He admired the piece, both stylish and functional. He saw little more up there, a few boxes, a chair pulled up to the desk, and a dark computer screen. But in the quiet he could hear the hum of the monitor.

"Did you set up this computer?"

"No." Her voice expressed some curiosity. "Maybe the movers did."

He sat down at the desk and waved the mouse over the wood. An e-mail screen came up asking for a password. They looked at each other. Someone had been on the computer.

"Do you know the password?"

She leaned in over his shoulder. "KKD603. They're our initials, Kevin, me and Delaney, and the date of our anniversary."

He nodded and entered the information. Messages began to blink onto the screen one after another.

"There's got to be hundreds of e-mails here," she remarked.

"Yeah," he replied grimly. "Keira I think the intruder may have been looking for something here, on this computer."

"Like what?"

"I'm not sure," he answered, concentrating on the screen.

She gasped. "Oh! I forgot to set the alarm. I want to do it right now, while I'm thinking about it."

"Okay, good idea."

She left and he studied the inbox. "It would probably be something that happened right around the time Kevin was killed," he said aloud, scrolling through the dates. *If* he was killed that is, and it wasn't an accident. He didn't know exactly what the date was, just that they were fast approaching the anniversary, so he started at the end of the previous December.

When he got to January eleventh, something caught his eye. "I think I've got something, Keira," he called out.

He heard her respond from downstairs, "What?" A few seconds later, rapid footsteps on the stairs announced her arrival.

"Well, I'm not sure if it's something or not, but on January eleventh, Kevin e-mailed himself some documents from work. I don't see that anywhere else. Is that something he regularly did?" He turned to look at Keira for the answer and found her face completely drained of color. "Keira? What's wrong?" He took her hand and found it cold and clammy. "Here, sit down." He moved out of the chair so she could get off her feet before she passed out.

"That was the date..." She broke off, staring blindly at the screen.

"The date of what, honey?"

"The date Kevin died."

Now it was his turn to feel a chill rush up his spine. He turned to ogle the screen. He moved the mouse to open the e-mail titled, "Max Gerardi's Papers." "It looks like some kind of bookwork."

"It's a stock report, probably prepared for a client. But why would Kevin have a stock report prepared by someone named Max Gerardi?"

"I'm not sure, but I think this is something we should let Detective Leake know about."

"I agree."

He made the phone call to Leake, but while he spoke, he kept watching Keira's face. She sat in the chair staring straight ahead, her hands gripping the arms, but otherwise unmoving. He hung up and squatted down in front of her.

"Are you okay?"

She didn't answer; in fact, it seemed to take her several seconds to focus on him. "Do you think this Max Gerardi guy had something to do with Kevin's accident?"

He ran his hand down her arm to comfort her. "I don't know, babe. Maybe."

"And this has been here...the whole time."

"You had no way of knowing—"

"Yes," she answered sharply. "But I should have gone through his things."

"Keira, up until last week you thought his death was an accident. Hell, it still could be an accident. We have no idea if this means anything."

"What did Leake say?"

"He seemed excited about it," Dylan admitted. "He wants me to send it to him so he can check it out."

"Well, here," she said, sliding out of the seat so he could sit down.

He typed in the address the policeman gave him and hit the send button. He studied her again. "I think you've had enough. Why don't we go downstairs?"

She nodded and they left the room, snapping the light off at the bottom of the steps.

"I think I'm going to have some Irish cream. Do you want any?" she asked.

"Sure." In her absence, he stared out the window.

She returned a few minutes later with two tumblers of ice and a bottle of Irish cream. She poured it without speaking and then they both flopped down on the couch next to each other, not even bothering to turn on the lamp. Dylan put his arm around her and drank, deep in thought.

"Did you get Delaney to your brother's house okay?"

"Yeah. She was beat. We don't go out on school nights very often..." Keira trailed off, but then she began to smile. "But we had a great night. She really loved the penguins."

"*You* loved the penguins," Dylan teased.

"I did. They're so cute."

"The polar bear exhibit was cool," he commented after a few seconds.

"I know. I loved how you could see them swimming underwater."

"Yeah, that was neat."

She rubbed his arm. "Dylan...do you think it's weird how close we feel already?"

He thought about it. "Sort of." He smiled. "But I'm not letting it bother me."

She chuckled, nestling in closer to him with a sigh. "I'm glad you're here."

"So am I." They drank their Irish cream in the dark until Dylan sat up with a jerk. "What time is it? It's got to be nearly eleven and you have to teach tomorrow."

"It's eleven-thirty," she stated after checking her watch.

"We need to go to bed."

"Okay." She stood and began to walk toward the bedroom. He didn't follow. After a few steps, she turned back around. "Aren't you coming?"

"No. I'm serious about sleeping out here."

A sly smile crossed her face and he could feel his palms beginning to sweat. "Really?" She sauntered toward him, holding his eyes, her gaze itself a sweet seduction. He held out his hands in front of him as if to ward her off.

"Na-ah. You are going to bed."

"You really aren't coming?" she asked, incredulous.

He shook his head, unable to trust his voice.

"Okay." She turned and headed for the bedroom, glancing back once with a look of disappointment.

With an exhale of breath Dylan sat down on the couch. *If she knew how close I was to giving in, she might have tried harder.* Resigned to his fate, he yanked a blanket from off the pile still on the chair and stretched it over himself as he lay down. *It's going to be a long night.* With a grunt he turned on his side, pulling the covers over his head.

CHAPTER EIGHTEEN

Keira gave up on sleep and turned her bedside light on. The man kissed her, and then went to sleep on the couch. The injustice of it. For the last twenty minutes all she had been able to think about was his kiss, and the way he'd made love to her the night before, how he looked in the parking lot at school, and the hardness of his muscles the first night when she so boldly climbed up onto his lap on the couch.

"Ugh!" She slapped at the covers in frustration.

Then two things happened at once to inspire her. Her eyes fell on her schoolbag, and she flashed back to Dylan's earlier statement of, "No funny business tonight...no matter how much you tempt me."

"Yes!" she exclaimed out loud. She covered her mouth with a giggle, pulling the covers back and sliding out of bed. From her schoolbag she produced the White Elephant gift she received when getting together with some of her girlfriends to celebrate Christmas. It was a sheer film of red, a flimsy excuse for a piece of lingerie, with a white faux-fur collar and a Santa hat to match. "Ho-ho-ho," she tittered in a whisper.

She slipped into the negligee and then surveyed herself in the mirror. Definitely a naughty little number. On a whim, she picked up a tube of lip-gloss and added a coat. She stepped back again. The red and black lace bra and panties she wore underneath hid what the nightie did not, but that just made it all the hotter. She was practically spilling out of the push-up bra and the panties, cut so high on the hip, with so little material elsewhere, showed her body off to a fine degree.

What would Dylan think? she wondered and worried, thinking of taking it off. But then, as she posed in front of the mirror, another voice said, *Think? The boy won't be able to think at all when he gets an eye on this.* Dared she?

With a wink at her reflection she took a deep breath and grasped the doorknob. Before she could rethink her idea, she opened the door and crept through the dining room. She could hear Dylan's soft snoring and chuckled, tiptoeing cautiously forward. He looked so cute lying there with his mouth hanging open. She sat on the edge of the couch and bent to whisper in his ear.

"Dylan?"

"Hmpf," he grunted.

"Dylan?" she coaxed.

He hugged the blanket closer and turned his back to her more. "Go away."

The wave of fury shot through her like water through a squirt gun. She grabbed a throw pillow, tossed on the floor, with both hands and beat him with it as hard as she could.

"Huh? What...?" He shot up so fast he dumped her on the floor.

"Dylan!" she cried out petulantly.

"What? Babe? Oh, did I knock you over?" He reached down and helped Keira to her feet. "What have you got on?" he asked, curious, and then, "*What* have you got *on*?" in a way which could leave no doubt the outfit had achieved its desired effect.

Empowered by the desire she saw in his eyes, Keira backed up, beckoning to him with a crook of the finger. "Santa told me you've been a *very* naughty boy."

"Oh, yeah." He made a lunge for her and she scurried out of his way with a squeal. She took off and he hopped over the trunk, rattling the tea set on it and nearly sending it to an early grave. About midway through the dining room he caught her. She screamed as he lifted her, kicking and laughing, off her feet.

She slapped at his hands. "You said you were sleeping on the couch."

"No way."

"You said—"

A loud *CRASH* sounded overhead. Keira yelped and they both stilled, trying to quiet their breathing to listen. There was a smaller tinkling of glass breaking, and Dylan set her on her feet. He started to move toward the door leading to the upstairs but she grabbed his arm.

"Dylan!"

He swung back to her and pressed a hand over her mouth. A floorboard creaked above them.

"Go out the back door and get to a neighbor's," Dylan whispered, his hand still covering her mouth. His jaw was set, eyes intense in the dark. "I'm not about to let anything happen to you now."

She shook her head.

He took his hand from her mouth. She tried to pull him away from the door.

"No, Dylan, no!" she begged him.

"Keira," he warned, his voice stern.

"I'm not going to leave you."

Footsteps sounded on the steps now. "Then go back to your room and lock the door," he ordered, breaking away from her and grabbing the bat that leaned against a dining room chair. He laid himself against the wall to the left of the door, the bat clutched in his hands, held at the ready. Her hands over her mouth, she shook her head back and forth, whispering, "No, *please*, no!" They watched as the white door knob turned. A man stepped through the door as it creaked open. He was holding a gun loosely in his hand.

The man's eyes grew wide as he caught sight of Keira, who stood frozen in place, staring at him. He straightened up. "Well, what have we here—" But he didn't have a chance to finish his statement as Dylan swung the bat at the intruder's midsection and connected, knocking the wind out of him. The assailant bent over double and the gun skittered across the floor. She scrambled after it and Dylan grabbed the stranger, closing his arms like a vise around the man's chest and arms.

Keira flicked on a light switch and stood, aiming the gun at the intruder, a determined expression on her face. "What are you doing here?" she shrieked, nearly hysterical. "What are you doing in my house?" Her hands shook with rage and fright.

"Keira," Dylan said quietly, and with effort she tore her eyes from the man to stare at him. "Easy with the gun, honey." He reached out toward her and then in a flash of movement Dylan pushed the man to the ground at her feet and took the gun from her quaking hands. He put one arm around her as he trained the gun on the man. "Are you okay?"

She nodded.

"Okay." The man on the floor made a slight movement and Dylan shouted, "Stay down there and don't move or I'm gonna blow your head off."

"Okay, okay, pal." He laced his fingers and put them behind his head.

"Keira, call the police."

She nodded and skirted around the man on the floor, giving him wide berth, to grab her cell-phone, which she spotted on the end of the mantle. Dylan watched their captive as she began to dial. Out of her peripheral vision she caught a motion right before hands grabbed her around her middle. The thief's partner had slipped out of the darkness and pulled her into him like a yo-yo. An edge of a blade pricked her throat.

"Put the gun down, son."

Dylan hesitated.

The man pressed the blade further into her neck drawing blood. "Put down the damn gun!"

He instantly put the gun on the dining room table, backing away with his hands in front of him to show he was unarmed.

"Ha. Shacking up with the paramedic, huh, honey?" he hissed in her ear. "Get up, Alan, you idiot! Get the gun." The man on the floor scrambled to his feet and took the gun from the table. "My stupid cousin, Alan."

DYLAN COULD SEE KEIRA trembling from head to toe and a sick feeling crept over him.

"Nice little nightie you got here, sugar," the gunman commented, running his free hand up her thigh and under the sheer curtain of material.

Dylan saw something ignite in Keira. She lifted her foot and viciously kicked her attacker in the crotch while at the same time sinking her teeth into the hand that held the knife. He screamed and doubled over just as two policemen charged through the door behind him. Keira ran to him and he stepped in front of her, putting one hand behind him to make sure she was safely covered. In seconds the officers had both men in custody without even much of a struggle.

"How did you know to come?" he asked Officer Leake.

"After I received the document you e-mailed me I realized the name, Max Gerardi, rang a bell. It rang a bell because I logged his name on the record of people seen in the neighborhood. I chalked it up to his having an affair with a neighbor when his record came back clean, but when you sent the e-mail, I knew we had our man. Then, on my way over here to check on the house before I went off-shift, a call came in telling us Mrs. Kelly's alarm was tripped. We got here, saw the tracks and broken window upstairs, and came in the same way they did, by climbing the tree out front."

His partner, who had the two men cuffed, facing the wall, presented Leake with the wallets he took from their pockets. Leake turned the second man around, "Meet Max Gerardi. He's a stock broker at D.L. Huffman & Associates where Kevin Kelly worked. I have a forensic accountant going over the document you sent me. I couldn't make heads or tails out of it, but I'll put money on it being evidence this one here played fast and loose with somebody else's money."

Keira stepped forward, and the anguish on her face made all the men forget for a moment everything else, even her outfit. "Did you kill my husband?"

Gerardi didn't answer, but his mouth fell open and he looked like he'd been struck.

"Did you kill Kevin because of...money?"

"I-I..." Gerardi stuttered. He couldn't take his eyes from her face. Dylan could tell that Keira made real to him just what he did, maybe for the first time.

"DID YOU KILL KEVIN?" Fury choked her words.

Gerardi seemed to recover and snapped his mouth shut, a hard gleam coming back to his eyes.

But his earlier reaction seemed to be admission enough for Keira and she put her hands over her face, breaking down. She bent her knees and curled into a little ball, wrapping her arms around her legs. All five of the men stood frozen, staring at the weeping woman, until Dylan stepped forward to squat down behind her and put his arms over her quaking shoulders.

Leake's partner stirred first. "Come on, let's go," he directed his captive, leading him past Keira toward the front door.

The confused man asked the police officer, "Did Max really kill someone?"

"Shut up, you idiot!" Gerardi growled.

As Leake led his prisoner out the door, the officer took one final peek at the huddled figures on the floor, before closing the door with a soft click.

He let her cry for a while and then scooped her up. He carried her to the bedroom. She wouldn't let him leave her side, so he curled up next to her and they fell asleep.

He woke at dawn, and not wanting to wake her, slid out of bed. At the door he turned back to gaze at her, struck again by her beauty. She still wore the silly negligee, the red film draping tantalizingly over the sheets. She lay on her side, hands curled up to her head and slipped under the pillows. She had cried all of her makeup away, but it didn't matter; she was still breathtaking. His chest was tight as he watched her, such a curious mix of innocence and sex-appeal. Backing out of the room, he shut the door.

Dylan stretched and decided to make a pot of coffee. He hunted around in the kitchen until he found the necessary equipment and got things started. Then he grabbed his gym bag out of the front room and took a quick shower. When the coffee was done, he took a cup into the living room and stood staring out the window. He replayed the last several days in his mind, from finding a bleeding Keira in her car, to collecting her weeping form from the floor the night before. The question she'd asked him rang in his mind.

Do you think it's weird how close we feel already?

It was odd, there could be no doubt. But he still couldn't shake the feeling that stole over him the moment he'd met her, the sensation he'd found the place where he belonged. With Keira and Delaney, he found his home. The strangest part was, he hadn't even known he was looking for it.

CHAPTER NINETEEN

Dylan pulled into the parking lot of the car dealership. He turned off the engine and shifted to face Keira. "Now here's the plan...."

She listened to his instructions attentively. She was grateful he came with her. Though tired of driving around in her brother's sedan, she put off car shopping as it was traditionally Kevin's field of play.

"...you let me do the talking. We have to act like we're not all that interested so we can keep the upper hand in negotiations."

She nodded obediently, but he sighed, seeming unconvinced she would follow through. He shook his head. "Okay, let's go."

A smarmy salesman attached himself to them the moment the showroom doors closed behind them. "This is our newest model..." he stated, going on and on about gas mileage and safety ratings. Dylan listened while Keira perched in the back seat, seeing how roomy it would be for Delaney. She couldn't help but be excited. She'd never owned built-in DVD players in any other vehicle. She ran her hand along the interior, then, noticed a tiny handle inside the door's window. Tugging on it, she pulled up a hidden sun shield which slid down into the door's frame.

"Oooh, look! There are these cute little window shades."

Dylan rolled his eyes, but the salesman immediately jumped on the statement, mentioning how nice it would be to be able to cut the sun and, he added helpfully, it kept the interior of the car cool in the summer. She gave Dylan a guilty smile. He shook his head, but chuckled and a warm feeling washed over her, the sense of being loved and cared for, something which had been absent in her life for what seemed like a long time.

"How about we take this little baby for a spin?" the salesman asked.

"Yeah. Sure."

"I've got the exact same vehicle out on the lot. I'll just go get some keys."

After the salesman left, Dylan leaned on the top of the open door's frame, peeking down inside at her. "Well you might as well come and try out this driver seat, you little goofus."

"I'm sorry. I just got...carried away...I guess."

He slapped her rear as she passed him.

"Ouch."

"I forgive you," he said sweetly.

She climbed behind the wheel and he crossed to the other side, getting into the passenger's seat.

"How are your displays? Can you read everything clearly?"

Keira checked. "Yep. I like the way this is set up..." She located the windshield wipers, so she could be ready for the snow outside, and the headlights.

"Check out this glove compartment. I've never seen one so roomy."

She glanced over. "Cool."

Dylan had a strange expression on his face.

"What?"

"I think you need to really check it out," he urged. "See how much space there is."

She cocked her head, observing him with curiosity. "O-okay," she answered slowly. She leaned over toward him and reached in, moving her hands back and forth. "Yeah. It's roomy all right," she commented, with raised eyebrows, still studying him.

She was about to remove her hand and lean back in her seat when he interjected urgently, "Hey, there's something in there."

She gave him a wry expression. "Really? It's probably a manual, genius."

The corners of his mouth jerked up. "I don't think so." He indicated the manual, which sat in his lap.

To oblige him, she felt around some more and her fingers discovered a small object in one corner. She pulled out a black ring box.

Her jaw dropped and she stared at it fixedly, her stomach plunging.

"Open it," he challenged.

"Dylan...?" Her voice held a nervous edge.

"Come on, open it," he murmured.

She placed her hand on the box, running a finger along the soft velvet. After a second she pulled back on the lid, which resisted at first and then popped open to reveal an exquisite diamond ring.

"Oh, my God!"

"Keira, I know this is crazy. It's crazy! It's absolutely insane." He paused, as if the whole thing were a wonder to him, too. "We've only known each other for a couple of days..." He gently clasped her arms. "But...it feels so right when we're together. I know we need to take some time to get to know each other better." He reached up and played with a strand of her hair for a second, but then gazed into her eyes. "But I want you to know that at the end of that time, I intend to make you my wife. That is," he added quickly, "if you'll have me. I can keep the ring for you until you're ready."

She took a deep breath. "I don't know what to say...I—"

Before she could go on to explain her own feelings, he jumped in. "This was a bad idea. I moved too fast. I've freaked you out. You're freaked out, aren't you?" He didn't wait for an answer. "I don't know what I was thinking! I should never have expected you to feel the same way I do."

"No, I—"

From out of nowhere, it seemed, the salesman showed up, knocking on the door behind Keira. She jumped in fright and the ring box flew out of her hands and into Dylan's lap. They stared at each other for a second and then he snatched it up and crammed it into his pocket.

"Ready for that test drive now?" the salesman asked, oblivious.

"Yes. Yes we are," Dylan answered brusquely, getting out of the car.

She sat stunned for a second. The salesman opened her door, but she didn't respond.

"She doesn't want to give it up." The salesman laughed.

"Yeah." Dylan seemed to force a laugh and turned away.

"Your chariot is right this way." The salesman led them to the exact same model on the lot, droning on and on about the different features the car had. Dylan nodded and added an, "Ah-hah," every now and then to the conversation, but she could tell he wasn't listening to a word.

During the entire ten-minute drive—the salesman insisted on Keira taking it out on the highway—Dylan sat with his jaw tight, staring straight ahead. She could barely concentrate on traffic. When they pulled back into the parking lot, she shut the engine off and turned her whole body toward Dylan.

"I don't need a test drive. You're right, it's crazy. It's insane. But that doesn't change the fact that it's right."

The salesman leaned forward slowly from the back seat, resting his hands on their chair's head rests and looking from one to the other. "We're not talking about the car here, are we?"

"It is crazy, but last night I realized I love you, Keira. I love you more than anyone. I love the way you belt out song lyrics in your car. I love the way your eyes light up when you see Delaney. I love the way you cried over the news story about the cruel way fishermen kill dolphins. I love the way you stood up to those men last night. You're one fiery redhead, you know that?" Before she could answer he continued. "And I love Delaney too. And, although I would never presume to try to take Kevin's place, I would try my best to set a good example for her, and I couldn't love that little girl more than I do. And—"

She leaned over and kissed him to make him stop talking and then pulled back to drink in his face as she began to speak. "My turn to talk now," she asserted firmly. "I did some thinking this morning, too, and I realized I had fallen in love with you. I was afraid you would leave me now Max Gerardi was arrested."

"Who's Max Gerardi?" the salesman questioned halfheartedly. They ignored him.

"So, I haven't scared you off?"

She grinned. "No way, pal." She kissed him and the tension released from his shoulders. "So what did you do with the ring?"

"Ring?" the salesman asked.

"Wait. Just wait one minute." Dylan got out of the vehicle and went over to her side of the car.

"What is he doing?" a voice asked from the backseat.

"Shh!"

He opened her door and then knelt down on one knee in the snow, pulling the ring from his pocket. "Keira, I want to spend the rest of my life getting to know you. Would you consider one day becoming my wife?"

"Wow!" the salesman cried, almost in the front seat now as he stretched forward to take in the scene.

"Shh!" Dylan and Keira hissed at the same time.

"You know, if a colleague came up to me and said, 'I met this guy a few days ago and now we're engaged,' I would think them either foolish or stock-raving mad! But that was before I met you. I mean, what can I say? When it's right, you just know it. You don't have to wait a legislated amount of time to know that. So, yes, I will marry you. I would be proud to be your wife."

He whooped and stood up to grab his fiancé. The two embraced in the snow, laughing and crying.

"Does this mean you want the car?" the salesman asked.

"Do you want it?" he asked her. She nodded. "We'll take it," he announced happily.

"Where's my ring?" she demanded.

"Oh, right here." He took it out and slipped it onto her finger.

She held her hand up to admire it in the car lot's lights. She threw her arms around him, squeezing her eyes shut. "Thank you, Santa."

Dylan sighed. "You bet!"

NOTE FROM AUTHOR

Thank you for reading UPON A MIDNIGHT CLEAR, part of my REAL ROMANCE COLLECTION. I hope you enjoyed it. Now that you've read the book, won't you please consider writing a review? Reviews are one of the best ways readers discover great new books. They don't need to be fancy or long, just a sentence or two honestly describing your opinion of/experience with the book. I would sincerely appreciate it.

Want more from M.J. Schiller? Page forward for an excerpt from:

TAKEN BY STORM

Book One in the ROMANTIC REALMS COLLECTION

TAKEN BY STORM

Bashea had gone to the well in the dark. She knew it was unwise, but it seemed so safe, just outside of the light from the fire where her family and other tribesmen sat telling age-old stories. If they had heard her scream, her brothers would have been at her side in an instant. The only problem was, her captors didn't give her time to scream. They were waiting, watching before she even lifted the handle on the gourd and stepped forward.

It all seemed so innocent. Her family was laughing, re-telling stories, ones oft repeated when they got together, like the one about her brother, Bagrat, and the camel. Bagrat meant "made by the gods," and, in Bashea's opinion, her brother believed he was. That was why the story about the camel spitting on him, just as he was about to ask for the hand of the woman who was now his wife, was so funny. Bagrat would always laugh good-naturedly and counter with a story about one of Bashea's other brothers, or something Bashea had done; there were plenty of those stories. They all would join in on the fun, talking over each other and repeating old dialogue word-for-word. Bashea possessed a wickedly fast tongue, and had so often stuck her foot in her mouth, it was permanently shaped to accept it. So, time and again, she was the one being teased when they gathered. Not that she minded; it was all part of being a big family.

It was this she was thinking of as she made her way to the well, feeling warmed by the comfort of kinship. It was cool outside the cozy ring of the fire, and Bashea was pulling her scarf tighter when they jumped her. Before she could even draw a breath, they took her own scarf and forced it into her mouth. She struggled against her attackers, but there were so many hands on her, she could not inflict the damage she wished to.

As they dragged her backwards, Bashea could see her father's face, lit by the fire, as he stood, the crowd laughing loudly at something he said. No one could hear her grunts or groans, or see how Bashea dug heels into the sand to try to slow the abductors. A short, squat man stepped into her line of vision, smiling evilly as he used a huge palm branch to wipe away the drag marks they were creating. The only signs left behind to point to her presence at all were a cracked gourd and a puddle of water.

The men brought Bashea to a camp, and then they really had their fun, each taking a turn with her until she finally passed out. Even then, they did not stop. When she would awaken, someone new would be over her, and Bashea would thrash about, fighting against the others pinioning her arms and legs. She used teeth to try to stop what they were doing to her, even head-butting someone, which had him drawing a knife to cut her arm in retaliation.

Bashea was sure they would kill her, or she would be abandoned in the middle of the desert, left to die. But in the end they rolled her up in a carpet, where she fought against the panic of suffocation, head giddy, lungs aching for air. Tossing her onto a camel, or some other beast of burden, it was hard to say which, they brought her to dump their load on the floor of a beautiful bedroom. With a brutal yank on the carpet, they sent her rolling out across the floor to the hearth, almost into the mouth of the fire that chased the chill from the room. Then they just left. She attempted to get her bindings off by various means, but finally fell asleep. On top of her exhaustion, the warmth of the fire lulled her. Besides, she needed to conserve her energy to fight off the next attack.

It was all so surreal. She wondered what her family must be thinking. They would have searched for her, if they had any idea where to start. But even she had no idea where she was. She knew her father would be very upset, and that pained her. She tried not to think about what the soldiers had done; it made her sick.

THE KING OF AVISTAD was dying, and there were those who wanted to hasten his death all the more. Young Prince Tahj knew this. He knew it as he was walking down to the throne room, his footsteps ringing in the empty hallway, his heart beating a mile a minute. The twenty-three-year-old prince had found that very thought weighing on his mind day and night since his older brother, Kadeesh, was killed in a war with the neighboring kingdom of Subda.

Tahj remembered the day he learned of Kadeesh's death. He was knocking around a cloth ball with his friend, Radeem, juggling it on his ankles and knees, when the messenger arrived. His mother's wail pierced through him, ripping a hole in his life that left Kadeesh on the other side of a great chasm. Kadeesh had been the brightest jewel in his father's turban, tall, with a bronzed, even complexion, radiant teeth, and a heart bigger than the very breadth of the good king's lands. He was a kind brother to Tahj, though six years his senior, and had always managed to spend time with the younger boy when he was home.

Since the fateful day Kadeesh was killed, the king had trained Tahj to take his brother's place as heir to the throne. Tahj accepted the mantle unwillingly; he did not believe himself to be the born leader his brother was. Maybe it was because Kadeesh was always there to lead the way; Tahj had become comfortable in his role as the understudy. And now, thrust into the limelight, he felt like a fool, strutting around and putting on airs he did not deserve. The place belonged to another. But, no matter what his feelings on the subject were, he knew it was his obligation to step up and bear the responsibility as best he could, for his mother, for his father, and for all of Avistad.

Tahj felt the little stab that had become so familiar whenever he thought of his brother and accepted the pain as he traversed the long hall, glancing up at the dozens of colorful, triangular banners rolling in the breeze off of the adjoining courtyard like waves in the sea. Light still streamed in, ducking between the pillars separating the courtyard at his left from the hallway. Though it was late afternoon, its rays still felt warm on his shoulder as he strode purposefully forward. It always amazed him that outside the thick walls of the palace, the sun could roast you alive, but within its shadowed walls, there was a chill that could never be permanently shaken.

As background music to his thoughts birdsong rang, sounding almost mournful as it ricocheted off the palace walls, coupled with the sound of a fountain somewhere nearby. The closer Tahj got to the throne room, the tighter his chest became, knowing any misstep on his part would be met by the derision of his father's counselors, especially the grand vizier, Lord Boltar. The man was a pompous ass, as far as Tahj was concerned, but he still wielded a lot of power, and so Tahj kept a close eye on him.

When Tahj entered the throne room and strode forward, he could already feel the others sniveling behind his back.

"Look, the boy prince has come."

"The fool!"

"He is not worthy to wear the royal turban."

Still, Tahj squared his shoulders and approached the throne, passing through the others as if swimming upstream.

The throne room was unnecessarily large, the back three-fourths of the room unused and in shadow. The only time these corners were lit was during a ball, when the whole room seemed to come alive as if it were put under an enchanted spell, broken only by the sound of music and laughter, and the tantalizing smells issuing from the kitchen just beyond. Now the room managed to smell both musty and, at the same time, like an odd combination of pine and jasmine. Columns sprang up in regular rows like soldiers, marching up to the bottom of a short but wide staircase that led up to his father's throne.

At the foot of the stairs, Tahj got down on his knees and bowed from the waist, his hands stretched out in front of him on the floor, as was proper, holding the position for several seconds before slowly rising.

"My son." The king reached out to clasp Tahj's hand warmly in his long, slender one. He was taller, thinner than Tahj, with steel-gray hair and a long, drooping moustache.

"Father," Tahj returned with feeling, stepping up and bending to kiss the ring on the king's hand.

His father was not looking well these days, he noted. His skin had taken on a gray pallor, and his hands shook uncontrollably. His golden robes hung from him, limp, as if suspended by the pair of hooks that were his shoulders. The older man coughed, the air rasping through his lungs like the clash of metal.

As the king fought to get his fit under control, Tahj slid his gaze to the group of advisors to his right, searching for the face of the grand vizier. He located the man with ease, his prominent red robes setting him off from the rest, his thin face looking strangely stretched, cheek bones and chin pointy under the dark, thin skin and smooth goatee. Was it his imagination, or did the minister's coal-black eyes seem to sparkle with menace, his thin lips lifting almost imperceptibly at the corners as he gazed upon the weakened king?

"You look well, Tahj," the king said, regaining his voice at last. "I take it things went well in Moleeda? You had no problem collecting the tribute there?"

Tahj turned from his scrutiny of Boltar and grinned easily at his father. "Things went well. The sultan sends his regards—"

"Aaaactually, Sire," Boltar interrupted, drawing out the word with feigned politeness, "I'm sorry to interrupt, Your Highness—" His voice was oily as he gave a slight bow in Tahj's direction. "—but the prince did not collect the entire tribute." He stood back, his arms crossed, a slippery smile splitting his face, above which his thin mustache twitched in anticipation of a conflict.

Tahj waited a beat before responding, his eyes like cold steel as he glared at Boltar. He returned his attention to the king. "This is true, Father, the sultan was a little short on his gold. He is in the middle of building a mausoleum to his late wife, and is drawing heavily from the treasury right now." Tahj glanced again at the grand vizier. "I believe, since he is grieving, we can give him a bit more time," he added pointedly.

"Sire." Boltar pounced. "This is exactly what I was speaking of. Everybody has a sad story they could share. If we allow people to go without paying tribute every time someone is ill or—"

The King waved a hand dismissively in Boltar's direction without even looking at him. "If Caspar says he will pay, he will pay. We've never had a problem with him. Was your travel pleasant, son?"

Tahj beamed, happy to have scored a point against his nemesis. "Very pleasant, Father." He chanced a glance in Boltar's direction. The grand vizier scowled, a vein pulsing in his elongated neck. "Very pleasant."

"Good, good. You must tell your mother and me about it at dinner, then."

Sensing he was being dismissed, Tahj clicked his heels together sharply and bowed. "As you wish, sir."

He left the throne room quickly, and was surprised to hear a second pair of boots accompanying him. A hand dropped over his shoulder. "It is good to see you, Prince Tahj. Welcome home. Your trip was good, then?"

Tahj tried to ignore the chill running down his spine. "Yes, as you just heard, Lord Boltar, it was good."

"Ahh...fine, fine. Well, we have a gift for you, the men and I." His tone was amused. "Something we brought back from a small village in the desert, just under the foothills of the mountains. Something to make you a man."

Tahj knew he meant a bottle of some strong drink. Unlike his men, Tahj rarely imbibed alcohol, and it had become a point of ridicule among the troops. "Thank you, Grand Vizier. I'm sure it was very thoughtful of you. Now, if you don't mind, I'm going into my private quarters now to open your gift." Tahj took the other man's arm from his shoulder as if it were contaminated and dropped it, turning to enter his room. The last image he had, as the door closed, was of Boltar rubbing his hands together with a sneer of sick satisfaction.

With a sigh, Tahj leaned against the door. "Like I would really drink anything *he* would send me," he said to the thin air. He straightened up and removed his short, robin's egg-blue, silk, beaded jacket, crossing through his sitting room to dump it on the curtained bed in his inner chambers. He removed his turban, too, throwing it unceremoniously across the bed. He hated the thing as it was both hot and uncomfortable. He only wore it for formal occasions or when conducting business, to lend himself an air of dignity his youth and inexperience robbed him of. He ran his hands roughly through his thick, black hair and then, with a loud, exaggerated exhale of breath, he flopped down on his mattress. Tahj worked to undo his loose blouse at the wrists where it was tied, at the same time tugging it out of the waistband of his tight, white, dress pants, also saved for formal occasions.

"Where is this dubious bottle of mead?" He glanced around the room at all the flat surfaces and saw no glittering bottle. Having freed his wrists, he dropped them to his lap as he continued to scan the room, realizing it felt good to be home in his own familiar surroundings. The brightly colored bedspread, the red drapes, the ornately carved bedside table, along with the spicy aroma of incense, all spoke of home. Light flooded the relatively small apartment from a wide bank of windows on the far side of the room, which still smelled of the fresh air he'd let in when he first arrived home. A crow cawed loudly in the courtyard off his bedroom, overriding the trilling of a warbler in a nearby acacia tree. A knock on the door interrupted his thoughts. He rose to open it.

With a cry of joy he pronounced, "Oh, ho, ho! Radeem, my friend." He was swallowed up by a large man with a wide, open face and hair as black as his own, who began to thump him vigorously on the back. "How good it is to see you. How long has it been?"

"Too long, Tahj...or should I call you Your Highness?"

Tahj laughed. "Oh, and am I, then, to call you Captain?" He snorted. Tahj had given his cohort the title of captain in his army a few years back. "Just Tahj will do. You are too much of a brother to me for it to be otherwise." He flung an arm around the taller man's shoulders. "Why are you back here?" he teased. "Missed all of the Avistad beauties, did you?"

"Well, assuredly yes. But that is not why I am here." His open face clouded. "Actually, Tahj, the reason I have come is rather serious."

Tahj couldn't have been more surprised. Something serious, from Radeem? Responsibility seemed to have matured him. "You seem troubled. Come in. Sit down." The two men grabbed the only chairs in the small parlor. Of the same dark, ornately carved wood as the bedside table, the chairs were high-backed and hard, with red, satiny, cushioned seats. A small round table separated the chairs, but the men were still almost knee-to-knee as each leaned forward to speak to the other.

Radeem glanced around. "You are certain no one is listening?" Tahj nodded solemnly. "It is bad, Tahj."

Tahj put a hand on Radeem's shoulder. "Tell me."

"It is about Kadeesh," his friend added hesitantly.

Tahj felt a lump rise in his throat, but nodded again in silence.

"I think he may have been murdered."

"What?"

Now he had begun, it seemed Radeem could not wait to tell his childhood friend all he knew. "He was not killed on the battlefield, like

Lord Boltar said. Kadeesh was found in his bed in the morning, his throat slit

Tahj knew he should be shocked, but he didn't feel all that surprised. He had known Kadeesh was too good of a swordsman to be killed by an untrained peasant, as reported. "How do you know this?"

"There is talk among the troops." Seeming to anticipate Tahj's objection to talk not being proof, he held up a hand, continuing, "But there is more. I'm afraid not only did Lord Boltar assassinate your brother, but he may also be preparing to overthrow your father. A friend of mine, a soldier, reported to me he was approached by two men and asked about his loyalties to the crown, and, although he swore his allegiance, he got the feeling it wasn't really the answer they were looking for. He told me they seemed disappointed rather than reassured. I asked him to describe the two men for me, and I am certain they were Boltar's men." Radeem stopped to study Tahj. "But you don't seem all that surprised by what I have to say."

Tahj rose so suddenly Radeem almost tipped back in his chair, but Tahj barely noticed. Standing behind his own chair, Tahj gripped the back as he spoke. "I've had my suspicions." He raised his hand to stop Radeem's interruption. "Nothing solid, mind you, it's just... I was afraid my own dislike for the man was coloring my thinking, but maybe I was right after all." He gazed off for a moment but then returned to his explanation. "He seems to undermine me at every turn. Every order, he questions; every mistake, he scrutinizes." Tahj threw up his hands, gesturing with each statement as he began to pace behind his chair. "And lately he almost seems vulture-like, as if he were waiting to swoop down and peck the eyes out of my father's corpse."

Radeem stood, too, his brow uncharacteristically furrowed. "I'm afraid we may have underestimated Boltar. His following may already be too strong. You know..." He hesitated. "...the rationing your father ordered was not a very popular move."

"Yes, but a necessary one all the same," Tahj argued. "Those people in the North were starving." The decision had cost his father many of his wealthy friends, friends who saw the rationing as simply money out of their pockets. And it was a decision that had made Tahj proud. "The floods washed away most of their wheat and barley crops along with many vineyards—"

Radeem put a hand on his friend's shoulder. "You don't have to convince me. I've always known your father to be a fair and intelligent man. But there are those who like to complain, and the rationing certainly gave them fodder to do so." The captain lifted his hands innocently. "That's all I am saying." Tahj nodded his understanding. Radeem paused, calculating. "I'm going to hang around here for a few months, keep my eye on things. I don't trust Boltar, and I want to be here if anything goes awry. Besides," he added, perhaps trying to lighten the moment, "there are those Avistad beauties you spoke of..." He let his voice trail off with a wide grin.

Tahj smiled and punched his friend lightly in the stomach. "You're all talk. I know you're quite pleased with that beautiful new wife of yours."

Radeem paused, as if considering. "You're right, I suppose," he returned with a sigh. "But I'd at least like to know I could find myself another wife, if I so desired. I haven't had a girl cast her eye in my direction in many a moon, my friend." He tapped his somewhat rotund stomach petulantly.

"Ohh, what a shame," Tahj commented, his voice dripping sarcasm. His smile spread. "Seriously, it is good to have you back, Radeem." Tahj took his friend's hand and placed his other hand on the captain's broad shoulder.

"It is good to be back," Radeem consented. "Now, I'm going to go spruce up for dinner. Maybe I can seduce some willing servant girl." He winked and headed for the door.

Tahj halted at the doorway. "You haven't changed a bit. Remember the time we snuck into that sultan's tent and you bedded about half his harem before he caught on?"

Radeem's eyes sparked, his laughter loud and robust. "Now *those* were the days." He sighed. "Still, I wouldn't change a thing. I do love my Aara." He shook his head. "I've turned into an old married sap. I never thought it would happen."

"Me, either," Tahj retorted mildly.

Radeem smiled. "I'll see you at dinner."

"Shortly, my friend."

Tahj closed the door on Radeem and turned to stroll back to his bed, absorbed in thought.

LORD BOLTAR WATCHED Prince Tahj enter his quarters and rubbed his hands together wickedly. He loathed the prince. He'd seen the boy as a toddler running naked through the castle. How could anybody be expected to take orders from someone after seeing that? And, damn it all, if Prince Tahj hadn't turned out to be a fairly competent commander on top of it. That fact alone had him grinding his teeth at night.

And before Prince Tahj it was Kadeesh. Kadeesh, well-proportioned, good-looking, and with an air of authority, even as a young lad; unlike Tahj, who spent most of his childhood playing games in his nursemaid's shadow. Kadeesh was a natural-born leader, and the King sensed it from the start. But royal blood ran through your fingers just as easily as peasant's blood, Boltar thought with a laugh. Kadeesh was no longer a problem. What people failed to remember was that Boltar, too, was once a prominent man around the palace. Before the king met and married his wife, it was Boltar he turned to for advice, Boltar whom he left in charge during his sometimes lengthy absences.

But, as soon as Kadeesh could walk, it seemed, Boltar's position in the palace diminished. It was infuriating. Boltar's father had been the grand vizier before him, and his father's father before that. In fact, somewhere in the past one of his family members had been second in line for the throne, and no one in the family had ever forgotten it. No, never forgotten. Boltar could still remember his father's deep bass voice reminding people time and again, "We're from royal blood, you know." Even as a young lad, Boltar was told someday the throne would belong to his family again.

But as it was, here he sat, keeping books while Prince Tahj went out to collect the tributes, which had been the Grand Vizier's duty in years past. Now, not only was he stuck behind in the palace, but he was also expected to manipulate numbers instead of people. It really wasn't his strongest skill, and it certainly didn't give him the rush of power he got when he was out dealing with the troops.

Boltar turned with disgust and headed away from Tahj's doors, still stewing. He hadn't gone far when his sharp eyes caught sight of a figure through the arched openings to his right, striding down the hall on the other side of the courtyard, facing the opposite direction. Radeem, he thought, sucking in a hissing breath. What would he be doing here? Boltar snuck behind a column and watched as the younger man met an intersecting crosswalk and changed direction. Radeem ambled through the courtyard which was sparsely covered with grass, the expanse broken up with tall, willowy trees and ornamental fountains, and approached the prince's rooms. One of the Grand Vizier's spies had warned him the captain had been asking a lot of questions lately. Was Radeem here to warn the prince?

Perhaps it was time to act. He'd planned on just a few more weeks to let the poison he gave the king do its work, but perhaps it was time, after all. It was just as well the current reign end in blood, rather than a quiet death. Besides being personally satisfying, it would also serve to establish Boltar as someone to be reckoned with. As Boltar thought about it, his pulse began to quicken. Nothing got his blood pounding faster than the rush of power he felt when torturing or killing someone. He turned, and as his heels clicked down the tile hallway, he ticked the next steps off in his mind.

ABOUT THE AUTHOR

M.J. Schiller is a retired lunch lady/romance-romantic suspense writer. She enjoys writing novels whose characters include rock stars, desert princes, teachers, futuristic Knights, construction workers, cops, and a wide variety of others. In her mind everybody has a romance. She is the mother of a twenty-three-year-old and three twenty-one-year-olds. That's right, triplets! So having recently taught four children to drive, she likes to escape from life on occasion by pretending to be a rock star at karaoke. However...you won't be seeing her name on any record labels soon.

ROMANTIC REALMS COLLECTION:

TAKEN BY STORM
AN UNCOMMON LOVE
LEAP INTO THE KNIGHT
LADY OF THE KNIGHT
A KNIGHT TO REMEMBER

ROCKING ROMANCE COLLECTION:

TRAPPED UNDER ICE
ABANDON ALL HOPE
BETWEEN ROCK AND A HARD PLACE
ROCK ME, GENTLY
MIDNIGHT MELODY

REAL ROMANCE COLLECTION:

UPON A MIDNIGHT CLEAR
THE HEART TEACHES BEST
DAMAGE DONE
HOMETOWN HEARTACHE
TAKE A CHANCE ON ME
BLACKOUT

DEVILISH DIVAS COLLECTION:

TO HELL IN A COACH BAG
DAMNED IF I DO
THE DEVIL YOU KNOW
SATAN, LINE ONE
PITCHFORK IN THE ROAD
SIN WORTH THE PENANCE

www.ingramcontent.com/pod-product-compliance
Lightning Source LLC
Chambersburg PA
CBHW061241170626
46809CB00007B/2772

* 9 7 8 1 9 3 9 2 7 4 3 4 2 *